TRUST

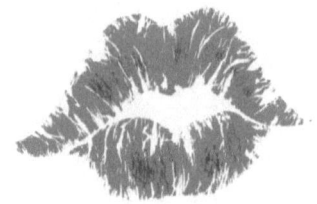

EVERNIGHT PUBLISHING ®

www.evernightpublishing.com

TRUST

TRUST

Trojans MC, 6

Sam Crescent

Copyright © 2016

Chapter One

One year from Mine

Daisy was in a fight, and Knuckles watched as the brother hit out at the other prospect. This was one of their many tests, and even Landon had been through this shit to become a full member. Standing beside him, Knuckles folded his arms and watched as the Prospect lashed out, slamming his fist against Daisy's stomach. It wasn't going to bring Daisy down. The prospect didn't have enough upper body strength, and really needed to work out more.

"The little fucker's not going to win," Landon said, biting into a hot dog toward the end.

"All you do is eat."

"Holly and Mary have been cooking up a storm for that food blog thingy. This bun is one of their creations, and fuck me, it's damn good."

"No one is going to fuck you," Zoe said, coming

up beside him. Zoe was Raoul's old lady, and had happened to become best friends with Landon during his prospecting. They had also been in college together. "You look ugly with the way you chew your food."

"Baby, leave the guy alone," Raoul said, coming up behind her.

Knuckles watched the couple interact, and Landon had this grossed out look on his face. "You guys are gross."

"What's the matter, Landon? Not happy to see love?" Zoe asked.

Knuckles tuned them out, concentrating on the fight that was going down. Daisy slammed his fist, and the Prospect spun away, landing on the ground. The fight was over as the guy failed to get up. *Rick, that was his name.* Rick the Prospect failed to get up, and that was the end of that fight. There was no victory. Daisy walked over, and with the help of several club brothers, they carried Rick toward the clubhouse.

"Did you hear we're bringing in a new piece of pussy?" Brass said, coming toward him.

"How are the other bitches handling it?" Knuckles asked. Whenever they voted in new pussy, the seasoned ones always had an issue. They didn't like other women screwing their men, and also, the men liked to test drive the newbies. Several of the club whores had decided to leave the club, finding love with some civilian, which they didn't mind. The club didn't force them to stay. They only demanded loyalty. Bee, Lori, Emma, and Lilah were still around, and several others.

It had been a long time since he fucked one of the free pussies that was available to him. A certain blonde with startling blue eyes stopped him at every turn. Bethany, or Beth to her friends, had come into his life, and now he couldn't shake off the need he had for her.

The fire in his blood wouldn't disappear. He wanted to fuck her, take her, control her, show her exactly how good it would be. The problem he had? She was Daisy's sister, which wasn't the only problem either. No, some fucker had date raped her two years ago, and it had made her skittish. Not only was that a problem, but there was also Daisy's belief that Knuckles was deep into the Dom/sub lifestyle, which wasn't exactly the case. In the past couple of months, he'd seen a change inside her. She no longer lived in the clubhouse. The apartment building where Crazy and Leanna used to live, Beth now lived there. She also worked in the Clinton Briars' office. Clinton was a lawyer, and she was now his secretary.

Knuckles had gone along with Daisy to make sure that Clinton knew to keep his wandering hands to himself. So far, nothing, but then Clinton had other women he was more interested in. Beth was more like a sister to the lawyer.

"You're not going to fuck this one either?" Brass asked.

"Not in the mood to get my dick wet."

"Boys are starting to wonder if your dick is ever going to get wet again. Do you even have one?" Brass leaned forward as if to look, but Knuckles swatted him upside the head.

"Back off."

"Dude, your dick is a muscle. If you don't use it, you lose it."

"You're giving me a biology lesson now?"

"Someone should." There were a few seconds of silence before Brass opened his mouth again. "You've got to move on. Beth's not ready for you."

"Fuck off."

"It has been well over a year. She not for you. Not to mention the fact she's Daisy's sister."

"Holly was Russ's daughter. He got over it with Duke, and Daisy will get over it with me." He wasn't backing down. Knuckles had known Beth wasn't ready. It didn't stop him from going by and seeing her.

Her apartment was filled with every part of her, her essence, her stuff. Every time he was there, he drank it all in, knowing it was enough for the time being. There would come a time when it wasn't enough, but he'd worry about that later.

"What's the woman's name?" Knuckles asked, showing an interest. He wasn't going to fuck her, but he could at least watch.

"Darla, she's twenty-five years old, and moved here a month ago. Diaz says her story checks out."

"And we're trusting Diaz with our shit now?"

"No, you're trusting me with this shit," Duke said, coming toward them.

"You're sitting in on it?" Knuckles asked.

Duke was seriously in love with Holly. Crazily so, as he'd even killed his first wife, who also happened to be the mother of Matthew, Duke's first son before Holly came along. "Yeah, I am. Holly's going to be there as well."

"Who's looking after Drake, and Bell?" Knuckles asked. Drake and Bell were their kids. Bell had been born in the last three months. The pregnancy hadn't been as hard as Drake's.

"Mary and Pike."

"Pike's missing this? He's the VP. Shouldn't he be here?" Brass asked.

"They've been having a few troubles lately." Duke turned away, looking around the back yard, probably for his woman.

Knuckles was aware of the problems between Mary and Pike. He'd stumbled onto them having heated words a few weeks ago, but it looked like there had been trouble in paradise for a long time. The couple had an interesting relationship to start with. Mary had had a crush on Pike. Pike had fucked her, and left her. Mary had been ready to move on, but ended up in an accident. Pike had come to her defense, we've all heard this story before. Of course, Pike wasn't happy with Mac, the guy who owned the diner in town, and happened to have a sweet spot for Mary.

Knuckles wasn't going to get involved in their lovers' quarrel. He had other important things to do. Holly rushed to Duke's side, and he paused to watch the couple as they kissed. Damn, they had been married for a few years now, and the romance between them hadn't died down, not one bit. In fact, it looked like it was getting hotter.

Finally, they broke apart, and Knuckles followed them into the clubhouse, about to watch Darla become the property of the club.

Taking a seat at Duke's table, Knuckles nodded to another prospect to get him a beer. Rick was still passed out, and Knuckles couldn't remember this guy's name. Barman, that's what he'd call him. The fucker was always serving at the bar anyway.

"I'm not sure I want to see this," Holly said.

"You wanted to see it, baby. I'm not touching her. You know that," Duke said.

"This your first time seeing this kind of initiation?" Knuckles asked.

"Yeah, and right now, I feel sick."

"The brothers won't rape her, Hols." Duke wrapped his arm around her shoulders. "You see this, and you'll understand. Any woman wants it to stop, or to wait, the guys back off."

"What will I see different?" Holly asked.

"You'll see the woman begging each man to fuck her," Knuckles said. "She'll be begging for it."

He'd taken several of the club women, including Lori. There was a time he'd loved this part, fucking a woman, and watching his brothers pleasure her. Then of course, he'd been involved in watching a few of the ceremonies with the old ladies, and there was just more. He didn't know about his brothers, but for him, when the brothers each took their own women, he felt like an outsider. Some of the women had been nervous, but the only guy they had wanted was right between their legs, holding them. There was this attraction, a connection that defied everything he'd ever known. He'd only ever been allowed to watch, never touch, never to feel what they were feeling, just a detached part of it all.

Darla came strutting in, swinging her hips. She was a nice woman, very sexy, very sensual, and knew exactly what she wanted. Walking right up to Brass, she stroked a finger down his back, and moved so that she was in his arms. He'd seen the move several times to the point that he wasn't affected by it anymore. Darla kissed Brass, trying to take the lead, but Brass was not known for letting any woman have the better of him. He pinned her against the wall, taking control of the kiss, consuming the both of them as he took what he wanted.

For a long time, Knuckles took what he wanted. He'd have taken Beth if only she'd given him a sign that she wanted it. He wanted her so badly, but she wasn't ready, not for him. Not yet.

****

Beth stared around the clubhouse. She had moved out, but she loved coming for the parties. Before crap happened with Benedict she had loved partying, being around people, and basking in that feeling. She wasn't drinking. No, she was standing in the back, watching as

Brass led a now naked Darla to the pool table. Prior to her attack, she'd loved to party. No one could get her away from a good dance and drink. Maria, her best friend, had hated it. Out of the two of them, Beth had been the partier while Maria had been the stay at home studier.

Now, Maria was the stay-at-home mom, and Beth was … something.

She wasn't part of the club, and yet she wasn't part of anything else. It had been a couple of years since her attack, and still, she couldn't bring herself to live. Living had failed her once before, and she didn't want to relive that experience. Glancing into the room, she saw Knuckles sitting at Duke's table, drinking a beer, and watching the show.

Looking toward the woman splayed out on the table, Beth had to wonder what he was thinking. Darla was fingering her wet pussy, sliding two fingers inside her cunt, and pulling them out to swirl across her clit. Even all the way over here, Beth heard Darla's moans. What would it be like to be that open with someone? Beth knew all about the club traditions, the way they took their old ladies, and the club whores. Leaning against the wall, she pressed her thighs together as she watched Brass cover his dick with a condom and then move toward Darla. He slid between her wet folds, covering the latex in her cream, and found her entrance. Slowly, he slid inside, and Darla gasped.

"Oh, baby, you're so big."

Keeping her thighs pressed together, Beth folded her arms as her breasts became heavy. She would love to be on the receiving end of that kind of possession, but there was only one man she truly believed she could trust more than anything.

Looking toward the table, she frowned. Knuckles

was missing. Where did he go?

"Do you like watching them fuck?" he asked, whispering the words against her ear. She hadn't even heard him come up behind her. When she made to turn around, he stopped her by banding an arm around her waist and holding her still. "Do you see how much she's loving Brass's cock?"

"Yes."

Beth sounded breathless, needy, and damn it, she wanted to be the woman there. Only, she didn't want Brass. She wanted Knuckles. He was the only one she wanted. The brothers of the Trojans MC had all built up her trust. She was Daisy's sister, and they wouldn't hurt her, not ever, she knew that.

Knuckles, he was different. He never treated her with kid gloves. In his eyes, she was Beth, not "Beth who was damaged", or "Daisy's sister". She was her own self.

"Brass is going to finish soon, and when he does, there's going to be another brother to take his place."

"How can the old ladies stand this?" she asked.

"Easy, none of their men touch the club whores. They don't need to."

Knuckles stroked her stomach, and she found herself closing her eyes as he touched her. The feel of his large hand against her made her feel safe. He protected her, and she knew no one else was ever going to hurt her, not now, not ever.

He was a large man, a fierce man. Looking behind her, she bit her lip as his dark brown eyes stared right down at her, going deep into her soul. He wouldn't let her hide from him. His hair was dark brown, and some had fallen across his brow, making her want to push it out of the way. Knuckles stood at over six feet, thick muscles … everywhere. She'd seen him lift a man up and throw him to the ground.

Now those arms were wrapped around her, and she didn't want him to ever let her go. Was she wrong to want this so badly? He called to her in ways no one else ever could.

Brass groaned, pulled out of Darla, and stepped away. Next Bertie took his place, and she watched as Darla took him without even batting an eyelid. She continued to finger her pussy, and Knuckles's hand moved down a little from Beth's stomach. She gasped and bit her lip, trying to contain her excitement of having him this close.

"No other man would ever be allowed to touch you."

"Really?"

"No. You'll be mine."

"If I don't choose you?" she asked.

He snorted. "Beth, you didn't have a choice from the moment you entered this clubhouse. The instant I saw you, I knew you were mine." Knuckles nibbled her neck, and she couldn't help but moan. He always knew what to do in order to drive her crazy. His words didn't frighten her. No, they aroused her.

Bertie finished, and then she watched as Landon took his place, sliding inside the new woman. It wasn't long before Pie came along, pushing his dick into her mouth, and Darla was begging for it, begging for them.

Knuckles pulled her back against him, and Beth felt the hard ridge of his cock pushed against her ass. The hand that lay low on her stomach went down to cup her pussy. She couldn't resist rocking on his hand.

"Tell me, Beth, is your pussy nice and wet?"

"Yes."

"I'm going to check. Tell me no if you want me to stop at any time."

She didn't want him to stop.

His hand moved up and slid inside her jeans.

Please don't stop.

Since moving out of the clubhouse she had missed this time with Knuckles. He always found a way to make her feel alive, and that was never going to stop.

"Well, well, well, look what I've found," he said, sliding his fingers through her slit. She gasped as he stroked her clit, running his finger across the nub, and sliding down to her cunt. Beth closed her eyes, shutting out the scene before her, and concentrating on the feel of his hands.

"One day soon, I'm going to have you on that dining room table I carried up for you. I'm going to make you spread your thighs open, and present me with your sweet pussy for me to eat. Once I'm done eating you, and making you come harder than you ever have in your life, I'm going to fuck you."

She wanted that, too.

"You're fucking my fingers, Beth, and I don't hear you saying no. You want it, too, don't you, baby?" he said.

"Yes." The word came out of her on a sigh. She wanted him.

"I miss you, Beth. I miss having you around the clubhouse. You just got your own place, and cut me out."

"I miss you, too," she said, not caring that she spilled her secret to him.

"This distance shit between us, it stops now."

"Yes. I wanted to prove to you that I had found my way. I was strong enough to go out on my own."

"Good. Now come for me." He pinched her clit then stroked her. Beth gasped, unable to contain her sounds as he brought her to orgasm. His free hand covered her mouth, muffling her sounds so that no one else heard her.

He didn't let her go until she was shaking in his arms, and desperate for more. She didn't want this to end.

With Darla's screams in the background, Knuckles pressed Beth up against the wall so no one saw her.

"I meant what I said, this distance and shit, it ends now."

"What about Daisy?"

"You just came all over my fingers. Whatever your brother has got to throw at me, let him. I'm not going to back down. I want you, Beth. You want me. Stop denying this shit."

Biting her lip, she nodded.

"I'll be around tomorrow night. Be ready at seven."

"What happens at seven?" she asked.

"I make you mine." He walked away, and Beth was shocked. She didn't know what to do or to say.

The man had just given her the best, and only orgasm of her life, and now he was walking away. Another man was fucking Darla, and Beth had lost all interest. She had come tonight to enjoy the party, but also to see Knuckles. There was no point lying to herself. He was the reason she found herself coming back.

"What are you doing here, little sis?" Daisy asked, coming to stand in front of her.

"Nothing. Where's Maria, and my niece?" she asked, changing the subject. *Please don't ask. Please don't ask.*

"She's upstairs waiting for me, and my daughter is with Mary and Pike. What are you doing here?"

"I came to enjoy the party."

"Beth…"

"Don't, Daisy. I can enjoy the party."

"It wasn't long ago that you were scared to come out of the room you were staying in."

"I've changed." She was much better. Having her own space, a job, a life, she felt safe, especially with her brother and his club near. Right now, she wasn't liking Daisy all that much. He was turning into a bit of an asshole. "Why are you all bruised?"

"Got into a fight. Stay away from Knuckles, Beth, I mean it."

"Stay away from Maria!" She folded her arms. "Oh, that's right, you didn't. You took what you wanted."

"What the fuck has gotten into you?" he asked.

"Don't tell me what to do. I didn't tell you."

"This is what this is about? You think you've got what it takes to win Knuckles?"

"Daisy, I love you. You're my big brother, but I didn't think you had what it took to be with Maria. I never for a second thought you were capable of really loving her the way she wanted." She shrugged. "I was wrong. If Knuckles is what I want, then you can't try to take charge."

"You think you want Knuckles? You don't even know him. He'd eat you up, and spit you back out."

Beth smiled. She moved toward her brother and gave him a hug. "You don't know me."

Chapter Two

Knuckles wiped down the body of the car that he'd just put back together. It was a piece of shit car, decades old, but the owner, Rusty Frank, loved it. He always made sure Rusty Frank was looked after. The old man had been part of Vale Valley since its bloody inception, or at least with the way he talked he had. Pushing ninety, Frank was always quick to tell them what they were doing wrong. At last count, Frank had over twenty grandkids, and even some great-grandkids.

"You're still working on Rusty's car?" Duke asked, coming out of the office.

"Can't help myself."

"You know it's a bag of shit, and there's a lot more interesting cars that could do with your attention?" Duke folded his arms, leaning against the car.

"Everyone always wants to work on a new car. Rarely anyone can appreciate the old classics, or bags of shit. What can I say? I like the bags of shit that no one wants, or thinks can't be fixed." He was starting to think that Duke was here for another reason.

"Daisy's looking for you."

"Ah, so he's a little pissed at me for chasing after his sister?" Knuckles wiped his hands on the cloth he had, annoyed with his fellow brother. Duke was just doing what a Prez was supposed to do, keep the peace within the club.

"What are you doing?" Duke asked.

"I'm showing a woman that she's not broken. Since when do you get involved with shit like this?"

"Shit like this is my responsibility. We've got a ride coming up in a month. Diaz is part of our crew, and we're transporting a shitload of product out of town away from us. I can't be having two men, two fighters at each other's throats during the whole ride. I've got a family, Knuckles. I'm not going to risk my life, or that of my club."

"I'd never put the club at risk."

"Yet you're going to fuck his sister."

"It's not just about a fuck."

"Then what is it about?"

Knuckles paused and smirked. "You think I'm going to tell you? You're my Prez, Duke, not my dad, and not hers."

"You're right, I'm not either of your dads. I'm the fucker that has to deal with the fallout if you two don't make it. If you're not sure on Beth, I'm the one responsible for Daisy coming and beating the shit out of you. When I went after Holly, I made sure I was fucking ready to claim that woman. She's mine, and no one is ever going to take her away from me. Russ was my club Prez, and I took his place with his blessing. Holly's his daughter. You don't think I know what the hell is going on here? I do. I've been through this, only I chose not to be a dick. Daisy's not her father. He's her brother."

Stepping back, Knuckles ran fingers through his hair. "What I feel for Beth is real."

"I figured as much. Ever since she came on the scene, you've barely touched any of the women."

"I can't let her go," Knuckles said.

"If you're serious about this, then go for it. Don't pretend, don't try to show Daisy you're this big man. Be the man, and make sure you settle all your differences before we head out on the road. I've got too much shit going on to worry about the two of you."

"I'll deal with it."

"Good."

Grabbing the paperwork from the table where his

tools were, Knuckles ticked through everything he'd done, making a note on all of the things that would have to be done in the future. The old car was going to be brand new in a couple of months. Knuckles had lost count of the number of engines he'd done on this old piece of metal. Still, a car is a car, and when you find the one you want, it's hard to give up, even if that same car has been changed enough to be classed as several different cars.

"How is Matthew getting on at college?"

Matthew was Duke's son, eighteen years old, nearly nineteen, and in college. He'd decided to go out of town to another state, so he only visited on every other weekend. Holly had wanted for Matthew to have choices even if he wanted to be a Trojan. If, after college, he wanted to be a Trojan, there would be a place for him to start to earn his patch.

"He's coming back next week, and we're supposed to go away with Drake. He's nearly four now, so he's getting nice and big, ready to start camping. Bell would be staying with Holly."

"I figured as much with her only being a few months old," Knuckles said.

"Matty has settled down. He's not the same kid that wanted to become a prospect before going away to college. The, um, the pregnancy scare last year really fucked him up. He's calmed right down."

Last year Matthew had had sex with a girl in his year, Luna Daniels, and the condom had broken. With Holly and Duke with them, Luna had taken a pregnancy test to discover she wasn't pregnant.

"Nothing like being on the verge of parenthood to wake you up."

Duke blew out a long breath. "I'm still too fucking young to be a granddad."

"You'd be one of those hot granddads," Knuckles said, laughing.

"Well, it's not happening, and I've got to be thankful for something, and that is the fact my son has gotten his head on straight. I can't deal with worrying about him. He's far enough away, and he's wise."

"You taught him to shoot, and to fight?" Knuckles asked.

"You got it. Every chance I get. My son is one tough nut."

Knuckles smiled. One day he hoped to be saying the same words. Not about the whole pregnancy crap, but about being a tough nut. He saw the love and the pride in Duke's eyes. Duke was a good dad.

"You wait until Bell is having all the guys chasing her. You're going to be the unbearable dad," Brass said, leaning against the wall, eating an apple.

"Leave him alone. Give him a chance to enjoy having a daughter," Knuckles said.

"Have you heard what Pike is planning? He's going to lock her up in a tower where she'll be too old to ever have sex or find men."

Knuckles burst out laughing. "Guy's kidding himself."

Moving toward the reception, Knuckles put the call through to Rusty Frank to come and pick up his baby.

"Excuse me," a feminine voice asked.

Looking up, Knuckles stared into a pair of green eyes. "What's the matter, sweetheart?" he asked.

"My car, it broke down, and I don't know what to do." She nibbled her lip, looking downright petrified. He didn't like women who were scared.

"Brass, need your help," he said. "You want to tell me where your car is?"

She made her way out of the door, and he watched as she ran toward the gate, and around the corner. There he saw a beat up old car with smoke coming out of the engine.

"You're not from around here?" he asked, waving a hand in front of him.

"No. I'm just passing through." She tucked some of her raven hair behind her ear.

Knuckles glanced behind him and was shocked to see Brass already there, but his usually mouthy club brother was fucking silent, drinking in the woman. Rolling his eyes, Knuckles moved his attention back to her. "We're going to need to push this toward the yard, but I can guarantee you're not going anywhere."

"Shoot, okay, there's no way I can get this fixed quickly? I don't know, use tape and glue."

"Sorry, no can do. Just from the smoke alone I can guarantee there's some problems there." Why wasn't Brass helping him with this? "Brass, you going to be any help?"

"Your car's fucked."

"Let's get it into the yard, and we can look."

All three of them rolled it toward the gates. The moment they came into view, Duke and several of the Prospects helped him to push it into position so he could have a look at it.

Opening up the trunk, Knuckles saw it was going to be no use. The engine was completely shot.

"When was the last time you had this thing checked out?"

"I don't know. I bought it a couple of days ago with cash," she said. "It was just the spur of the moment thing. Jump in, drive, explore."

Staring at her, Knuckles didn't like how jumpy she was. "I need some ID."

"Really?"

"Yeah, really."

She grabbed her card out of her back pocket, and he saw she was twenty-eight years old, Eliza Bishop.

"I'll be right back."

Heading into the office, he put a call through to Raoul. "I need you to do a quick search on Eliza Bishop. Raven hair, twenty-eight years old."

"Something going on?"

"Don't know."

"Give me a minute. I'll call Diaz."

Taking the phone with him, he placed it in his back pocket, and made his way back toward Brass and Eliza.

"Is everything okay?" Eliza asked.

"Your engine is completely shot. Whoever sold you this piece of shit, they didn't exactly do you a good deal. I'm going to have to do you a whole new engine, and that's not even including the mess underneath the car, pipes and shit."

"Ugh, I just really wanted to get on the road."

"Any reason you running?" he asked.

"I'm not running."

Brass sent him a look, but he wasn't interested in having a brother playing mute, like a television.

If he wanted to stay silent, then he could fucking remain so.

The phone rang, and it wasn't Raoul. It was Diaz.

"Hey, brother, chick is fine. Raven hair, chunky, fat tits, full ass, that kind of thing?"

"Yeah," Knuckles said.

"She's not running from the law, more like her family, and responsibility."

"Rich?"

"Loaded. They own some kind mechanical

company. It originally was shipping, and it has just expanded. All you have there is a rich piece of ass who's trying to run from Daddy, and marriage is all."

Staring at Eliza, he saw it. The clothes she wore were not cheap fabrics, but expensive. "Fine, thanks."

"No problem."

Hanging up the phone, he stared at her. "You're going to have to wait for your car to be fixed. There's a perfectly good hotel in Vale Valley, or you can use the motel just out of town. Your car will be ready in three weeks," Knuckles said.

"How do you know it's going to be that long?" Eliza asked.

"Because I fucking said so, and building a new engine takes time, and I have to order the parts. Now, do you want the work done or not?"

****

Beth glanced down at the skirt she wore, which came to her knee, along with the plain white crop shirt. It was hot, and she didn't have a clue where they were going, so how was she supposed to get dressed?

The entire date, or whatever it was Knuckles wanted from her, was stressing her out. Pushing her hair out of the way, she quickly tied it up in a ponytail, and jumped as he knocked on the door. Out of habit, she checked to make sure it was him first.

You can do this.

Opening the door, she smiled, and then paused as she took in the cool box at his side, along with another bag.

"Hello," she said, drawing out the word. "What is that?" She pointed at the bag and box he held.

"This is our date."

"Our date is in a box and a bag?"

"Actually, Holly and Mary are trying this new

thing on their food blog. Showing how to make a great first date amazing, and with these recipe cards, along with a whole list of equipment you'll need to make it all a success," he said.

"I love Holly and Mary, and their blog is adorable."

"I happen to tell them what I had planned for tonight, so they wanted me to be their first experiment of how it went. I have pasta, sauces, chicken, and seasonings, along with the makings for a luscious dessert. Oh, and I also have some sappy romantic comedy. All guaranteed to make a great first night."

She was oddly touched by the experimental date. "You've already hit a snag."

"What?"

"You've got to give me a reason to let you through the front door." She raised a brow, resting against the door, and covering the gap with her weight.

"That's easy." She gasped as he pulled a rose out of his pocket. He took a step toward her, and pressed a gentle kiss against her lips. "May I please come in, Beth?"

"Yes."

She stepped out of the way, giving him room to pass. Her lips tingled from that single touch. Knuckles went straight for the kitchen, and she followed him, holding onto her single flower. The single rose, it meant something to her.

"Can you actually cook?" Beth asked.

"I can cook. Most of the time I chose not to. However, since Holly and Mary realized that I could do it, they keep giving me these little experiments to see how I get on. The other month I produced an intense chocolate cake that was so damn light and fudgy at the same time. Yeah, I'm a girl. I ate the whole thing."

Beth laughed, imagining a large man like Knuckles finishing off a cake quite easily. "I eat too much cake. I'm hoping being away from the clubhouse and Holly and Mary's cooking, I'll be able to lose some weight. I've always been too fat."

Knuckles spun around, slamming his hands on the table and glaring at her. "You are fucking beautiful."

"Knuckles?"

"You don't need to change for me. I like your ass just fine the way it is."

"It jiggles." Her cheeks heated at just admitting her body wiggled.

"So, it'll give me something to hold on to when I'm fucking you. Nothing wrong in that."

She covered her cheeks. "Sometimes you shock me with what you say. There's never any filter."

"Baby, filtering shit will only hurt others in the long term. I say what I mean, and I'm not nasty when I do say shit. Some stuff you don't say, and other shit you do." He shrugged. "No more putting yourself down, or talking about going on diets in my company, got it?"

"Got it."

He went back to emptying his bags, and she took a seat at the table. "So, um, what are you going to make?"

"Well, that will be answered in this card, right here." He held out a card and started to read. "Okay, we're having a pesto chicken pasta with a chocolate soufflé."

"Wow, that doesn't sound hard at all."

"Don't worry, baby," he said, pulling out a bottle of wine. "You're going to have a glass of this, and relax. We're going to chat. Nothing stressful about that."

Beth hesitated. She hadn't had a drink since that night that changed her whole world. *Why are you refusing? Knuckles would never hurt you.*

"It's up to you if you want a drink, Beth. I'm not going to force you. I'm not going to hurt you."

Biting her lip, she stared at the bottle of red wine, and nodded. "I'll have a small glass."

"Again, you don't need to have a lot." He got a glass out of her cupboard and poured a generous amount, handing it to her. She held it in her hand, sniffing into the glass at first.

Instead of drinking, she merely held the glass in her hand, and smiled at him. "What was going to be your idea of a date?"

"There's a little picnic spot up near by the lake." Knuckles smirked. "I actually caught some guy there from another MC."

"Is it dangerous?"

"Nah, he was just having some quiet time, nothing to worry about. I was checking it out a few days ago. I wanted to take you there. That was what I *was* going to do."

"Holly and Mary have other ideas?"

"I tell you, those women could get anyone to do anything. They're deadly."

"Do the others know that they get you to cook?"

"Not a chance. I'd rather die than admit I'm a sucker like this."

Once he had everything spread out on the table, Beth took a sip of her wine, and slowly found herself relaxing as he worked the ingredients. He diced up vegetables, throwing them into a baking dish, seasoned them with spices, herbs, and olive oil, tossing them around before placing them in a preheated oven. Next, he worked on the chicken, seasoning it up, and putting it to one side.

She enjoyed watching him cook, his hands

moving so swiftly and efficiently. He prepared the ramekins for the chocolate soufflé. Before she knew it, the glass was empty, and she was reaching for the bottle again, pouring them both a glass of wine. He put the finishing touches to the tray of baked chicken, and cooked the pasta. Once the chicken was out, he let it rest, and immediately placed in the chocolate soufflé. Her mouth was watering.

Throughout it all, they had talked about Holly and Mary, and how successful their blog had become.

"Now, my lady, our dinner awaits." He put a plate in front of her, and the scents were just sublime.

"This smells so good."

Cutting into the chicken, she gathered up some spicy sauce and took a bite, moaning as she did.

The sound of a cell phone going off made her look toward Knuckles. He smirked. "They want to know how it goes."

She moaned again. "This is divine. If I'd known you could cook like this, I'd have had you around more often."

"Why do you think I used this as my initial date?" He winked. "No one can resist a man that cooks."

"Very true."

He put his cell phone away. "How are you finding Clinton?"

"The guy I work for?"

"Yep."

"Um, it's just a job. He's very demanding, and requests excellence from everyone around him. I don't believe he's ever lost a case, and he hopes to keep it that way."

"He can be an asshole."

"That too. People don't hire him to lose." She respected Clinton. He was a hard-ass who made sure he won. He knew a variety of different laws, and as such, his office offered several different kinds of lawyer. If someone came into his offices needing advice or a lawyer for an area that Clinton wasn't part of, then he found the next available man for the job. He was a businessman, a competitor, and offered much more than many lawyering groups. It was what shocked her that he chose a small town like Vale Valley to conduct his business.

When she asked him, he always said that Vale Valley was in his blood, and he didn't see a reason to abandon what he loved and what he knew. She couldn't fault him, not really.

"You respect him?"

"He's many things, and he's a great boss. I don't see a reason not to respect him." She finished her dinner, moaning at the last bite. "Do you not like him?"

"It's not about like. He's got a bit of a reputation with the women in his life."

She chuckled. "I know. I've seen them coming into his office, all thinking they're the ones that are going to snag him. They never do."

"Always keeping them at bay?"

"Always."

"Let's enjoy dessert."

Beth poured them another glass of wine as Knuckles finished serving up dessert. Taking the spoon he offered, she placed it inside the light soufflé, and took a spoonful. It was beautiful.

"This is the best food I've ever had."

"Good."

Once the food was finished and the dishes washed, they made their way toward the television. The bottle of wine was left on the table, and Beth changed to soda. She wasn't interested in getting drunk, and she felt happy with herself. Having a few glasses of wine was a victory for her. Of course, she doubted if she would have been able to do with without Knuckles there. He made her feel safe.

He placed his arm along her shoulders, and within minutes she was resting against him. Knuckles kissed the top of her head, and she couldn't help but think about the feel of him his hands teasing her pussy.

Her nipples grew hard, and she closed her eyes, trying to bring her body into focus. Knuckles ran his hands down her body, creating so much sensation as he touched her bare arm.

"You haven't touched me tonight," she said.

"I know."

"I thought you would."

"I'm not in a rush to end something this good between us. I want you to learn to trust me, Beth. It's not about rushing you into fucking. We're going to take it slowly."

"Why?"

"Because I'm not an asshole."

"You fingered my pussy last night."

"I know. It's not going to happen tonight. This isn't about rushing you." Glancing up at him, she saw the sincerity in his gaze. "Believe me, Beth, I want to bend you over, and fuck you so damn hard that it hurts. Anyone else, I'd have done that. I want you to feel me everywhere, to be everywhere for you."

"You are."

"Then let's keep it that way." He kissed her head, which only served to frustrate her. Even though she was somewhat frustrated, she couldn't help but smile. This was what always made Knuckles different. He was so patient with her, never willing to rush, and yet, like last night, he had the ability to surprise her.

Chapter Three

"Are you working on my car?" Eliza asked.

Brass looked up from where he was ordering the parts to stare at the woman who had dumped a piece of shit car in their garage. No, he couldn't deal with cars. He was the one who tended to handle the business side, ordering what was needed, and take payments. Rusty Frank had been by thirty minutes ago to pick his piece of shit up.

"No."

He didn't like the way he was feeling when he was around this woman. This was their second encounter, and words were failing him. It wasn't like she was a celebrity or a porn star that he might have beaten off to a time or two. What was it about her?

"Oh."

"We have to order your stuff first."

"You don't have anything waiting around in the back?" She gave him a smile, but he saw it was forced. There wasn't even an ounce of flirtation about her, which he found … weird. Most women he'd come across loved to fuck with a bad boy. Now, this woman, she looked ready to hightail it out of there. Of course, it could have something to do with the fact she was a fucking loaded. A princess with daddy's plastic.

"Do you know the first thing about fixing a car, or do you only ever rely on what your father can do?" he asked.

She visibly paled. "You ran my name?"

"We've got our ways."

"Will my dad know that you ran my name?"

"No. We have people who specialize in being discreet." Diaz always made sure his searches didn't alert any authorities. "You running?"

"No, I'm not running."

"Then why were you afraid of Daddy finding out where you were?" he asked. Why was he asking all of these questions? He didn't give a fuck, not really. She was a woman, and he could have anyone he wanted. There was a full club of waiting pussy at the clubhouse.

"I'm not afraid. I just don't want him to be here. If he was, he'd find a way to convince me to do what he wanted rather than what I wanted."

Folding his arms, his curiosity got the better of him. "What does he want you to do?"

She sighed. "You already know I come from a wealthy family, I don't see why I should pretend. He wants me to do what every single father wants their daughter to do. He wants me to marry the guy he's picked out for me."

"What do you want?"

"To not get married. It's stupid, but I actually want to live my life a little first. See new things, experience new things."

"This is what you're doing, breaking away?"

"Yeah, I guess I am. Or at least I'm trying to break away. I don't know. Every time I've tried it in the past, he's always found me. Him, and the guy he wants me to marry." She ran fingers through her hair, and he caught the tattoo decorating up her arm. It looked like interwoven black leaves, very dark, yet beautiful at the same time.

"Give Vale Valley a chance. It may surprise you."

"From what I've heard, there's an MC."

"Ah, you've already heard of us." He smirked. Trust the townsfolk in the diner to let her know who to look out for.

"Us? You're a Trojan?"

"Trojan MC, proud and happy. This shop is owned by the club. The guy who's dealing with your car, he's a club brother as well. You also met the Prez yesterday. He was working on some of the bikes that were in the shop."

"Wow, um, I didn't actually anticipate ever meeting an MC."

"Why not? We're not dangerous." He smiled. "Most of the time, that is."

"Are you flirting with me?" she asked.

"Honey, I flirt with everyone. Like I said, take a chance, and stick around. You may find your rebellion staring you right in the face."

Brass stared down at her full body, knowing he'd gladly show her exactly what he'd do with her. His cock pressed against his pants, and he wanted her, badly.

He would wait. The interest was there, he saw it.

Soon, he'd see how far his little miss prim and proper would go.

****

Matthew sat in his old room feeling somewhat disconnected from it all. He'd been at college well over six months, and even though it was great, it wasn't home, nor was it high school. Fuck, he wasn't homesick. Nah, he'd grown up a lot since he'd been here last, and since he wanted to join the Trojans. He was still going to do that. Trojans were in his blood, and one day he'd do everything that was needed to prove his love and loyalty to the club.

Opening the draw next to his bed, he removed the single picture he had of her, along with the bag that he had placed the pregnancy test. Luna Daniels. She had unwound him, and showed him exactly what it meant to be a man. He'd fucked her over in more ways than one.

They had been study partners, and he'd taken the next step, screwing her in the back of his father's pickup struck, taking her virginity. He'd hurt her as well. Thinking back to that moment when he slid into her tight pussy, he'd been in heaven, and she'd been in hell. Gritting his teeth, he ran his thumb across her picture, wondering what she was doing, who she was doing.

He'd fucked her, hurt her, and moved onto the next available pussy without a care for what it did to her. The condom had broken, and he'd warned her but hadn't expected anything to come of it. When she'd come to him to say that her period was late, he'd been scared shitless. He was too young to have a kid. Then of course as he started to think about it, he rather liked the idea of being a father. Luna was amazing, and he really did care about her. Most of the guys at school hadn't seen how great she was. They'd been too hung up on her size. She'd been all curves, and he liked curves. Before his dad started screwing Holly, Matthew recalled having a hard-on about her. Once she became his step-mom, it had taken on a completely different direction. No fucking way was he ever going to beat off to his step-mom.

At the time, he'd wanted that kid more than anything. He already planned to marry Luna, even if she didn't like him. When she'd come out of the bathroom, shattering his entire world, Matthew hadn't known what to do. He pretended to not care. Once his parents left, he'd gone in and found the pregnancy test, placing it inside this plastic bag. It was probably wrong of him, but it meant something to him at least. No one else would ever know what it meant.

Luna wouldn't talk to him. He didn't tell anyone what happened, and they seemed to go back to school, having nothing to do with each other.

Damn, he missed her.

A knock at the door had him putting everything away. He rested his hands on his knees and called for whoever it was to come in. Holly peeked her head around the door.

"You've been up here a long time. Duke's waiting for you. So is Drake."

"I'll be down in a minute." He ran fingers through his hair, looking around, wishing for something … more.

"Are you okay?" she asked.

"Yeah, of course."

"Yeah, of course—you don't sound so convinced."

"I've just got a lot on my mind."

She came in and closed the door. "I saw Luna the other day."

His heart started to race.

"Where?"

"Around town. I tried to talk to her, but she seemed a little uncomfortable. Did the two of you ever talk about what happened between you?"

"No. We didn't. It just happened, and then, nothing." He cleared his throat, wishing the questions would stop.

"You care about her?"

"I don't know—"

"Matthew, before you thought you got her pregnant, you were an asshole like most guys. Going around screwing everything you could get your hands on. I got it, I didn't like it, and I thought your respect for girls in general was pretty damn poor." She held her hand up as he went to talk. "But you're different now. You've changed. I don't know if it's the baby scare, or if you actually liked Luna. Getting pregnant, it changes people. It changed your father, and it changed me. It changes everyone. If you see her, or when you see her, stop, talk."

"If she doesn't want to? It's not down to if I don't want to talk. I can't make her talk to me."

"You're Duke's son, Matthew. Make her talk to you, and I don't mean violence. Just be your charming self, and before she realizes it, there she is, coffee, a cinnamon bun, and a conversation." She patted his knee. "Think about it. Otherwise you're going to spend your whole life looking back to this moment, wondering what could have been."

"Do you ever look back?" he asked.

"No. There's not a moment I regret. Don't make your life about regrets either."

****

"So, how was it?" Mary asked, coming toward him with Starlight, her daughter, trailing behind her. They were both covered in chocolate, and when he entered the clubhouse kitchen, he saw the counters laden with chocolate brownies.

"What the hell happened here?"

"We're testing out a variety of brownies for our blog. Also, I can take them to the diner."

"Daddy hates it when you go to the diner."

"Shush, Star," Mary said, smiling.

Knuckles looked at Mary's flushed face. "Is that what is causing all the problems with Pike?"

"It's nothing."

"Pike hates Mac," Starlight said.

Knuckles chuckled. "Where's Holly?"

"Matthew came in early, so she's staying behind to see them off. She'll be back with Bell in no time. Are you going to tell us what happened?"

"Here are the rest of your ingredients. It went down amazingly well, all things considered. Beth wasn't expecting me to cook at her place, and we watched the movie as well. It was … good."

Mary squealed. "That's great."

"Hold on, I said it was good."

"Which means great to me."

"How?"

"Are you going on a second date?"

"Yeah."

"See, we made her comfortable with food and a movie. Beth's not like a lot of women. You want her to get comfortable around you. Don't go blasting her with whatever you had planned."

"I was going to take her for a picnic up by the lake. The secluded spot near the trees."

Mary paused. "Nah, it would have been sweet, but it was filled with promise of more."

"How so?" he asked.

She turned to her daughter and asked her to go find her father, waiting until Star was out of earshot before speaking. "It's simple. A quiet, secluded picnic with a sunset. Just the two of you, a blanket, conversation, alone. It would lead to something. Beth, she needs to have a slower, more frustrating approach."

Knuckles sat down after pouring himself a coffee, thinking about it. "I could have put too much pressure on her?"

"Precisely. You don't want to pressure a woman. It makes us skittish, and when we become skittish, we tend to want to find a reason to bail." She shrugged.

"Taking that in, last night was a huge success. I'm picking her up tonight. We're going to see a movie."

"Good. Dinner afterwards?" Mary asked.

"Yeah."

"Taking things slow is always good."

Knuckles agreed. He picked up a brownie and took a large bite, tasting the hint of chili, and not finding it offensive. "These are quite good."

Pike entered the kitchen with Starlight on his hip. "She was sent to find me." He kissed her cheek, blowing a raspberry.

"Relationship convo is all," Mary said. "We can get tucked into brownie-making now." She turned around and started working on the chocolate she was cutting up.

Starlight wiggled out of her father's arms and rushed toward her mother. Taking his coffee and an extra brownie, Knuckles left the kitchen, only to find Pike left straight after, following behind him.

"Wow, you're not going to handle that?" Knuckles asked.

"When you have problems in your marriage, you learn when to walk away."

They made their way out toward their bikes. Knuckles took a seat on the wall, basking in the warm summer sun.

"So, trouble in paradise?" Knuckles turned toward Pike. "You cheated on her?"

"Fuck, no." Pike visibly recoiled. "What the fuck makes you think that? She tell you that shit?"

"Nope. Just your woman turned her back on you, and there was a time you fucked everything. Just an initial hunch."

Pike snorted. "I wonder if it would be easier to just fuck someone. Maybe she can see it from my side."

"Your side?"

"Her and Mac, they're getting close again, okay? To the point that five times last week, I had to pick her up from his diner, and she thinks I'm pissed off because I didn't get sex. She hasn't got a clue that she's so fucking beautiful, and Mac wants her." Pike paused, shaking his head. "I thought he'd get one of his own women by now, but no. He's still there with mine."

"Are you sure?" Knuckles asked. Mac had once had a soft spot for Mary, but that was years ago. Then again, he did give her half the diner, and also she had the control over the menu. Maybe there was something going on, or at least, Mac trying to create trouble in paradise.

"Yeah, I'm sure. I've got my own dick. I know when a guy is trying to take from me, and it's not happening. Not today, not tomorrow. Mary is mine."

He watched Pike straddle his bike, with clearly the intention of going to settle a score with the diner man.

Knuckles took another bite of his brownie, thinking back to last night. It really had been a perfect date.

****

"So, my brother let you out of his sight for two minutes to come and see me."

"It's not like that, Beth," Maria said, smiling.

Holding little Tanya, Beth stared down at her sleeping niece, falling in love with her all over again. She was such a sweet girl, so loving and quiet. "I know it's not like that."

Maria and her brother had an interesting relationship. Beth was aware of Daisy's need for control. It wasn't a violent control, or anything like that. It was something a bit deeper. She couldn't be sure of it either, only that Maria had flourished being with him.

"She's so cute," she said.

"And she sleeps through. I never thought she would. There were times I thought she'd, you know, be a bit of a problem, but no. She's a darling."

"Are you taking care of yourself?" Beth asked. "I've heard that some mothers can struggle in the early days of giving birth."

"I'm not in the early days of giving birth, Beth. I

know what you mean. Post natal depression. I know, Daisy was worried, and he made sure I was okay. I'm more than fine. I'm blissfully happy."

"That's good." She was happy with her best friend. Maria had chosen to come with her to Vale Valley rather than go off to college. Maria was like a sister to her, and now she was her sister-in-law, so it all made perfect sense.

"What about you?" Maria asked.

Glancing up, Beth frowned. "Me?"

"Yeah, you. I'm happy. I'm in love with an amazing guy. I have a beautiful daughter. I'm an old lady in a wonderful MC. What about you?"

"I'm happy."

"How are you coping?" Maria asked.

Her best friend knew everything, and had been there to help her afterward. Maria was her rock, where she had been dying inside. "I'm fine. I, um, I had a date last night with Knuckles."

"You did?"

"Yeah, don't tell Daisy. He'll ruin it for me."

"He doesn't think Knuckles is good for you."

"I told him to butt out of it." Beth shrugged. "I don't know. I want to move on. It has been over two years now. Can't I move on? Am I not allowed to move on?"

"Benedict won't ever be able to hurt you again, Beth."

"I know. I should have been stronger though."

"You did what you had to do."

"At what cost? Are there other women he's going to hurt in that way?"

"I know your brother and several men went to pay him a visit. I doubt they'd let him hurt anyone else."

"Or they all run away, hiding like it was all their

fault."

"It wasn't your fault, Beth."

"I don't know. Some people would argue that I was the one in the wrong for going to the party in the first place. I shouldn't have gone."

"I should have gone with you. If I had, I'd have been there to keep an eye on you."

Beth sighed. "I fucked up, Maria. I just, I want a clean shot. A chance to actually be happy, and that's never going to happen if I don't move on. I like Knuckles. He makes me feel … alive."

Maria smiled. "Daisy makes me feel that. Everything is always so dark before he comes into a room, and when he's there, the world falls away."

"That's the way I feel with Knuckles. Our date was sweet. Did you know he can cook? And you can't tell anyone else that. He cooked for me, and it was so delicious. He put me at ease."

"Daisy's going to be annoyed. He's asked for Knuckles to leave you alone."

"I'm happy that he's ignoring him. It's my life, no one else's, and even though I love my brother, it's not his place to tell me what to do."

"He cares, and he worries."

Beth sighed and glanced down at the Tanya who wiggled in her arms. What would it be like to have a child of her own? She wondered if Knuckles wanted a baby. He'd make one hell of a dad.

Chapter Four

Knuckles rubbed the back of his head as he glanced over at the beautiful woman by his side. The movie they had seen was heavy on the erotic. There was a time he had to wonder if he hadn't taken her to a full-fledged porn film. He'd wanted to take his time, allow her to get used to him, and instead, the movie had been a complete disaster.

They walked side by side, and he listened to the other movie goers, talking nonstop about the film.

"When I get you home, I'm going to try that out on you," one guy said.

"So," Beth said, surprising him by actually speaking first. "Was that intentional, or just coincidence?"

He looked over at her to find that she was smiling. Her cheeks were slightly flushed, and she looked on the verge of laughing. "You know it was coincidence. I read the review, and it was supposed to be cultured, a love story."

She snorted. "I've seen more love with Darla getting initiated into the club."

"You snorted. I can't believe you're laughing."

"You're squirming, and you look seriously uncomfortable. Why?"

He shoved his hands into his jeans and shrugged. "I don't know. I don't want you to feel like I'm pressuring you."

"It was an … interesting movie. I don't feel pressured, not at all." She chuckled. "Please don't act like you have to wear kid gloves around me. It's bad enough that I get it from Daisy and from Maria."

Knuckles paused, and they both stopped, moving

out of the way so people could pass freely. "I don't."

"Then why were you nervous? What happened to me, happened. I can't change it, even if I wanted to." She held her hands up. "Please, be Knuckles. Be the guy who doesn't care what happened. See me for a person, and not for anything other than that."

Knuckles reached out, stroking her cheek. "I don't."

"Then don't think a silly movie would make me think less of you. After what you did to me in the clubhouse, you better be taking some pointers."

She pulled away, laughing as she started down the street. He loved the fire inside her. This woman, she'd changed in the months she'd been at the club. Beth was stronger, harder, yet more confident within herself.

"Baby, I don't need any pointers."

"Really? Nothing left to learn."

"Nothing. Ask me anything, and I'll tell you."

"Hum, interesting." She linked her arm through his as they made their way to the diner, which was still open. "I can ask you anything about sex?"

"Anything." Knuckles doubted there was a single thing she could ask.

"Okay, did you know you were going to do that to me in the clubhouse?"

He smiled. "Do what?" If she wanted to get right down and personal, he was happy to do that. However, he was going to make sure she said things right.

"You know."

"No, I don't. I did a lot of things. I watched your brother fight, a Prospect get his ass kicked, a slut get fucked. You name it."

"You touched me." She slapped his arm.

"If you're going to be asking me questions about my sex life, don't you think you should be able to actually say it?" he asked.

"You're right. Did you plan to stroke my pussy?"

He tripped over his own feet as she surprised him with her choice of words.

"Ha, see, I can surprise you."

"Baby, you're treading in dangerous waters."

"Well, did you?"

"Plan it?"

She nodded.

"Not a chance. I didn't plan anything when it came to you. I saw you. I saw the way you were looking at Darla, and I just couldn't look away from you."

They got to the diner, and Knuckles found them a booth in the back. He didn't want any disturbances. They grabbed their menus, scanning over them. He took his order first, and Beth had the same.

He liked a woman with a good appetite.

Pouring her some water, he watched as she folded her arms in front of her and leaned forward.

"Tell me, what was going on in that head of yours while watching Darla?"

Her cheeks turned a wonderful shade of red. "You really want to know?"

"I wouldn't have asked if I didn't."

She signed. "I thought I was supposed to be the one to question you on all things sex."

"You are. I can ask some of my own."

"Fine. I found Darla … freeing."

"Freeing?"

"Yeah, she wasn't plagued by bad thoughts. She looked completely in the zone, and almost lost, headily on arousal. I've never felt anything like that, and yet, she could feel it without even thinking, not really. There was a room full of men, and most of them, they wanted her. They wanted to screw her."

"You want that?" he asked.

She shook her head. "I don't want a room full of men to line up to fuck me. I want to feel that safe within myself to express that kind of need. I've never known that, and I feel like I shouldn't feel that, if it makes sense. If you take away what happened to me, okay, think about the way women have to be in the work place, or to even get equal rights." She leaned forward a little more, and he found her passion inspiring. Fuck, she was actually turning him on. "I read somewhere that women in the porn industry, just as an area, they don't even get equal pay. They have the same sex that men do. They're getting pushed around, flipped over, banged around, and forced to swallow some nasty stuff, and they don't even have equal pay within a scene."

Knuckles smirked. "Do you watch a lot of porn?"

"Seriously, out of everything I just said, you're hung up on porn?"

"Every guy loves a little bit of porn, especially when their girl likes it as well."

She held up her finger. "I didn't say I liked it. I just happened to read it. For all I know, it was false, but then, women overall are paid less than men in exactly the same jobs."

"I agree with everything you say. Any woman that is doing exactly the same job should be paid the same. If that woman is doing a little more, then she should be paid more."

During the entire conversation, Knuckles wondered if Beth realized how close she had gotten to him. They were practically touching lips with how close they were.

"Here is your order," the waitress said, and they both pulled away.

"This looks great," Beth said.

"Enjoy."

The waitress was gone, and Knuckles gritted his teeth. Of all the worst times to actually invade his personal space, she had to pick now.

"You're looking mightily ticked off there. How come?"

"Nothing." He grabbed a cheese soaked fry and popped it into his mouth.

"Nothing? I thought it was because we were interrupted from having our little moment. I was expecting a little kiss, or something." She looked up at him, smiling wickedly.

"I'm starting to think that you've been hiding this little minx."

"I may have." She shrugged. "There's no telling, is there?"

Knuckles sat back, watching her. He had heard from Maria that Beth used to be a bit of a wild, party animal. Now, he was starting to see little signs of her rebellious personality. She wasn't this scared, timid little girl. She was in fact an outgoing woman. What had made her seem so timid was what had happened to her.

"I enjoyed going to the movies with you. It has been a long time since I enjoyed myself like that, going out, having fun. It was great."

"Vale Valley is having a good impact on you."

"I don't know. Maybe it's being around you, knowing my brother doesn't want me to."

"I should take that as an insult. You're only with me because of your brother."

She giggled. "Not really, no. To be honest, I want Daisy to see that I'm growing up, and I'm better, if that makes sense. I didn't have an illness, and like all scary things, it takes some time."

"I'm glad you're happy."

"So, will you be taking me on another date?"

He picked up his cheeseburger and took a large bite. The special sauce was something Mary had implemented for Mac's burgers, and it was so damn good.

"I don't know. Are you free tomorrow night?"

"Sure, I'm free."

"Cool, I want to take you shopping."

"Really? You're a guy, and you're offering to take a woman shopping. You do know that it's a crazy idea to invite a woman shopping?"

"It's not for clothes. I've got something I want to get you."

Knuckles smirked when he saw her confusion. He loved watching Beth, the way she worked shit out, all of it.

"Huh, okay, so we're going shopping, but it's not for something I need, or maybe even want?"

"You'll never guess, which is why it's going to be so much fun to take you."

"Will we be riding on your bike?" she asked.

"No. I'm afraid this is going to have to be by car."

"All right," she said, smirking as she took a bite of her burger.

They ate the rest of their food, enjoying conversation. By the time they were finished, the diner was ready for closing, so Knuckles walked her toward her apartment building. He didn't stay outside, but walked her right up toward her door.

"This is me," she said, joking. "You can come in for coffee, or tea, or even a beer. After sharing wine with you last night, I went shopping."

"Should I be worried that you're turning into an alcoholic?"

"Not at all. Or maybe? I can't seem to remember half my date."

He cupped her hips, and pulled her forward, pressing a kiss to her head. "Goodnight, Beth," he said.

"Oh, um, goodnight."

"I enjoyed tonight, Beth."

"Me too. I really did. Thank you."

He waited until her door was closed before leaving her building and walking toward the clubhouse. When he entered, he found Daisy sitting at the bar with Tanya in his arms, drinking from her bottle.

"Are you waiting around for me?" he asked.

"What do you think?" Daisy glared at him. "You know, I asked you as a friend to stay away from my sister, and yet you're dating her."

"Beth has a right to make her own decisions, Daisy. If she didn't want to go out with me, guess what, I wouldn't force her."

Daisy snorted, and immediately calmed down as Tanya got a little scared.

"You really shouldn't be having this conversation with me right now. What is going to happen is between Beth and me, no one else."

"She's my sister, and she was fucking date raped."

Knuckles gritted his teeth. "That's all you see, isn't it?"

"What the hell are you talking about?"

"There's more to Beth than what happened. You need to fucking see it." Knuckles shook his head. "I'm not going to have this out with you."

"Daisy?" Maria said, coming downstairs. She was wrapped in a gown, and she took the two of them in, biting her lip as she did.

"Yeah, baby," Daisy said.

"Beth's happy."

"She's my sister. I know what is best—"

"No, you don't. You don't have a clue what is best for her. You're only going on what *you* think is best," Knuckles said, getting angry. "Why don't you go and see her for yourself? Maybe then you'll finally realize that I'm not going to hurt her."

****

Beth hummed to herself as she put the latest files away into the filing cabinet. After last night's date, she'd gotten a good night's sleep, and even though she'd been worried that Knuckles had gotten into the habit of kissing and going, she knew it wouldn't last.

"Someone is in a perky mood this morning," Clinton said, coming out of his office.

"Sorry, I didn't mean to distract you."

"You didn't. I'm just waiting for a client to come in for a drunk and disorderly." Clinton folded his arms, leaning against her desk. He blew out a breath.

She chuckled. "You sound troubled."

"It's nothing. Ugh, okay, fine. I've met someone, only it was a friend of a friend."

Beth held her hand up. "You're coming to me for relationship advice?"

"You're the only woman here, and I don't trust anyone else. Is that a problem?"

"It's not a problem. I don't consider myself an expert."

"You're a woman."

"Okay, fine, hit me with whatever you want to say."

"I met this woman, and she's really sweet. She works in a bakery in the city."

"All right. I still don't see the problem right now."

"It's not a problem. Look, I'm an asshole. I accept that I'm an asshole. It's who I am. I have to be. No one should like me, and women, I bed them, and forget about them."

Beth pushed her hair out of the way. "So?"

"I like her, and the thing is, I was going to say all these shitty things to her, only I didn't."

She chuckled. "What's her name?"

"Rebecca Duncan."

"I never thought I'd say this, but it sounds to me like you've got some feelings for this woman."

"I do, only she doesn't think I want anything to do with her."

She frowned. "I'm confused."

"Rebecca told me at the end of our date that she doesn't want me to feel pressured. I went out with her because of our mutual friend. I don't know how to get her to want to go out with me again."

"Ask her."

"What?"

"Call her up, and ask her. It's the best way of getting her to go out. You're not even waiting for someone else to do the honors." She patted him on the arm, laughing. "You look a little shocked."

"I'm the lawyer, and I didn't even think about calling her up and asking her."

"You're welcome."

The bell on the door rang, and she turned to see her brother entering.

"Oh, dear, brother of mine, have you been naughty?" she asked.

"Not at all."

"Really? You're entering a lawyer's office, and you think you've been a good boy?" she asked, teasing him.

"Seriously?"

"What?" she asked. "Why would you be here at exactly twelve o'clock?"

"I wanted to take you to lunch if you're free."

"Believe it or not, I am free. It's lunch. Do you want me to bring anything back?" she asked, looking at Clinton.

"Yeah, sure, I'll have a cheeseburger. Make sure it's loaded."

"Will do, champ."

She grabbed her bag, and followed her brother out into the hot midday sun. It was moments like this that she was pleased that Clinton installed some air conditioning.

"What's going on?" she asked.

"Why does there have to be anything going on?"

"I don't know. I've been working for Clinton for awhile, and this is the first time you've come to my work place. I'm a little nervous. Have I done something wrong?"

"Not at all. I just wanted to treat my sister. Nothing wrong in that."

Beth paused and stared at him. "This is about Knuckles, isn't it?"

The smile on Daisy's face disappeared. "You shouldn't be dating him. I wanted to spend some time with you, and just talk, please. Let's go and eat."

"Did Maria put you up to this?"

"I love you, Beth."

"That wasn't in question." She knew Daisy loved her, as did both of her parents. Beth knew how much love they all had for her. Maria was like a sister to her, and the club women had opened up their clubhouse and their homes for her.

They entered the diner, and she saw Mary

working the front desk. She gave her a wave and gave her Clinton's order. Taking a seat close to the door, Beth stared at her brother.

"Knuckles, he's not all that he seems."

"Okay, fine. Why isn't he all he seems?"

"He's got a dark side to him."

She closed her eyes, rubbing at his temples.

"With women, he has to have all the control. He's the Dominant person in a relationship."

"From what I heard, so are you."

"He likes whips and chains."

She gritted her teeth. "Just come out with it."

"Knuckles is a Dom, Beth. He likes submissive women, and he gives them strict orders."

Beth stared at her brother. "That it?"

Daisy frowned.

"Yeah, I know what Knuckles is, Daisy. I've seen his stuff, actually."

One night when they'd been talking in the rain, he'd taken her back, and as he was getting something out of his closet, a large box of BDSM equipment, paddles, clamps, whips, dildos, had fallen out. She had asked him about it, and he'd been honest.

This was what she loved about Knuckles. He was completely honest. There wasn't anything else with him. He'd also told her that it wasn't something he *needed,* but something he enjoyed doing, that was all.

"Why didn't you start by asking if I wanted this kind of relationship? Why didn't you ask how I felt?" She shook her head. "You're my brother, and I love you very much. You don't trust me to make decisions like this. I like Knuckles."

"You don't know what you want."

"Really?"

"Beth, you're not in any mind to make that kind

of call. You were terrified of being around men—"

"Shut up!" She growled the words out and leaned forward. "What happened to me was my business. I know you took me in, and I know you care about me, and you're worried, but don't tell me what I should, and shouldn't feel. I don't like it."

She got to her feet and asked Mary for that burger.

"Is everything okay?"

"Yeah, I've lost my appetite."

Daisy moved up behind her.

"If you still want to have a friendship with me, then I suggest you think about what you say." She was so damn mad. What did Daisy think? Did he think she was just going to fall for anyone who showed her interest? Even before that damn party where her life changed forever, she'd never jumped at just any guy who looked her way. The very fact he thought that pissed her off.

She paid Mary, and left the diner with Daisy right behind her.

"I care about you, sweetie."

Spinning around, she pointed a finger at him. "If you cared about me you'd have asked me about what I think, and about what I feel. Instead, all you're doing is telling me reasons why I shouldn't be with a guy I actually want to be with. Unless you start treating me like a sister, don't come near me again."

She stormed into the office and handed Clinton his burger.

"Everything okay?"

"No, it's really not."

Beth finished her day at work and made her way home. She was so angry still.

Her mother had called to ask her how she was, and she'd told her about Knuckles and about Daisy. Her parents missed her, but she wasn't about to head back there. It was no longer her home, and it hadn't been her home for a long time.

Entering her apartment, her own small space, she went straight to the fridge, and grabbed the bottle of wine.

Pouring herself a large glass, she growled as the doorbell rang. She was going to start tearing the damn thing off. With her glass in hand, she went to check who it was.

"Are you here to break up with me?" she asked, seeing Knuckles.

"No. Why would I?"

"I had a rather unpleasant visit from my brother. I figured if you're here, it's because he tried to get into your head, and now you want nothing to do with me."

"I'm not the kind of man who gets told what to do."

"No?"

"No. I'm here because we had a date."

She stepped back and waited for him to enter. "You're not going to stop seeing me because of my brother?"

"Daisy's my club brother. He's got a right to be concerned, but when it comes to me and you, his fears are unfounded."

"He tried to tell me about you being a Dom."

"And?"

"And I told him I already knew. There was no need to warn me because I knew."

Knuckles smirked. "I bet he had a field day with that one."

"I don't know what I'm doing here with you, Knuckles."

"We're having fun."

"We're not having sex."

"I'm aware of that. I didn't say we would be having sex."

"I don't think I could be a submissive."

Knuckles sighed. "Stop worrying about that shit. I'm not asking for one, and you don't need to be scared."

He opened his arms, and she went to him. Wrapping her arms around him, he held her close. He made her feel safe in his arms, and she never wanted to leave that feeling, never.

"What is it?" he asked.

"Don't let me go."

"Never."

**** ****

Mary was so tired. It was late, and what she hated more than anything was the fact she didn't want to go home. She wanted to see her daughter. Starlight was everything to her. What she didn't want was Pike trying to push her around. He wasn't mean or abusive. His words stung much more. He didn't trust her, and she found that much more upsetting than anything else.

She could go back to the diner where Mac was, or she could walk into her house, and deal with whatever the fuck was going on with Pike. Closing her eyes, she stepped forward, and the door opened.

Opening her eyes, she saw Pike standing there, leaning his weight against the doorframe.

"You're late."

"I walked home."

"Mac's not even making sure you get home now."

She sighed. "So we're going to fight again. Why? You know I love working at the diner. You know I love you."

"You're working with a man who has feelings for

you, Mary. You're not just going there for a few times a week. You're there every single day."

"It's my job."

"No! Your blog is your job. The diner, it was a way for you to make money, and you haven't needed it for a long time. Mac hasn't moved on, and I'm not going to risk him taking you away."

"You don't trust me."

"Of course I trust you."

"If you trusted me, you wouldn't even be worrying about me. Instead, you *are* worrying about me." She took a step toward her home. "Can I come in? Where's Starlight?"

"She's in her room. I put her to bed. She asked after you."

They were turning into awful parents. She was spending more time at the diner, and he was at the club. Starlight was going to nursery, and between them, they were passing her backward and forward.

"We can't keep living like this," she said.

"Quit."

"No. I love working."

"You love working more than spending time with me."

"Look what is happening to us, Pike. You can't stand for me to be working. Your jealousy is tearing us apart. I don't doubt what you're doing at the club. I know there's no other woman there. That is trust. Why can't you give me the exact same trust?"

Pike closed the door, and she stared at his back.

"I want you to do as I've asked. I want you to end things with Mac and the diner."

"Nothing is going on." The diner was a good way of experimenting, of testing their ideas on the locals' palates. She even put on the menus every week the experiments, and she gave them all cards so they would give her feedback. She placed her hand on his back. "I love you."

"It's not good enough."

Tears sprang to her eyes. "You don't trust me. I'm sure you've warned Mac not to try anything."

"How would you feel if I spent most of my working day with Lori? Emma? Lilah? That wouldn't bother you?"

"Well, yeah," she said.

"Then think about it from my point of view. You know what, fuck this." He grabbed his jacket and stormed to the front door.

"Pike?" She rushed toward the front door, and there she watched as she straddled his bike, and rode away.

He'd left her.

She was alone.

"Mommy?"

Wiping away the tears, she smiled up at her daughter. "It's okay, sweetie." She didn't have a clue what to do, but she'd figure it out.

Chapter Five

Knuckles sat with Beth, his arm across her shoulder. When he had taken her shopping a few days ago, he'd intended to buy her a kitten or at least a puppy. What he hadn't known was that Beth was allergic to both cats and dogs. So, he'd bought her a new mixer instead, which now sat in pride of place on her kitchen counter.

The moment they had entered the pound, she'd started sneezing, and it had only gotten worse.

"I love this," she said.

He stroked her arm, leaning in, and smelling her hair. Knuckles loved late nights like this where he got to hold her.

Her hand rested on his thigh, and it took every ounce of willpower not to move. His dick was rock fucking solid, pressing against his jeans, wanting close to her. He wanted close to her. For the past week, make that the past year and a half, he'd been beating off to thoughts of her.

Staying still, he teased her hair and waited for the feeling to die down. Then he happened to feel the tips of her fingers stroking inside his thigh. Unable to deny the feelings consuming him, he glanced down, and saw she was indeed stroking his thigh.

"Beth?"

"Please," she said.

He couldn't do it, so he stood. Daisy's words came back to haunt him, and he hated his fellow brother in that moment. He wished he could have beaten the shit out of him.

"We were supposed to be watching the movie."

"Knuckles, we've been dancing around this for so long. I'm ready."

Pressing the heel of his hand against his eyes, he shook his head. "You don't know what you want."

Removing his hand from his eyes, he stared in amazement as Beth stood. She didn't wait for him to say anything. She lowered the dress she wore, and it fell to the ground in a pool at her feet. She wasn't wearing a bra, or any panties. How the hell had he missed that?

"From the moment I turned up at Vale Valley, we've danced around this." He watched as she licked her lips. "I know you want me. I see it right there in front of me. I guess my brother got to you. It's a shame."

She lowered herself to the sofa.

"Beth?"

"So, I'm going to show you what I want."

Words were hard to come by when she leaned back on the sofa, spread her thighs, and placed her feet on the cushion so he had a perfect view of her cunt.

"Beth?"

She ran her fingers through her slit, and he saw she was soaking wet.

"This is what you do to me, Knuckles. We don't have to have sex, and I love spending time with you. I just ... I want more."

He moved toward the coffee table, taking a seat. At the same time, he loosened his jeans and pulled his cock free, sighing.

Her gaze went wide. "I had no idea you were that big."

"Don't worry, I'll fit."

She chuckled. "I'm not worried about that. I know you'll fit."

Running his hand from the base of his cock up to the tip, Knuckles couldn't look away from her pussy. She was completely naked, exposed, and he loved what he saw. He couldn't wait until he got his hands on her curves.

What's stopping you?

Moving away from the coffee table, he knelt in front of her, inhaling her pretty pussy.

She didn't stop him. Flicking his tongue out, he slid it across her tight clit, and she gasped. She tasted so damn good that he slid his tongue down to her entrance, plunging inside her to get more of her on his tongue.

"Fuck me, baby," he said.

"I want you to."

"Soon."

Pre-cum leaked from his tip, but he didn't want to be touching himself. Releasing his dick, he ran his hands up her body, cupping her large tits, and teasing the pink tips. She was so soft and curvy. Pinching her nipples, he groaned as she arched up.

"Sensitive?"

"With you, yes. Everything feels alive, as if I can't help but feel. It's amazing."

"You're amazing, baby." Holding the weight of her tits in his hands, Knuckles knew he was going to be sliding his tongue between that valley soon enough. He was going to mark every inch of her glorious body, and then some until she had no doubt who she belonged to.

Moving down, he ran his fingers over her rounded stomach, then dipped between her thighs, spreading her lips, which were covered in her cream.

"Are you horny for me, baby?" he asked.

"Yes, please."

Sliding two fingers inside her, he groaned at how tight she was. He was going to need plenty of lube to make sure she wasn't in any kind of pain. Knuckles wasn't a small man, not at all.

When it came to Beth, he wanted her panting and yearning for it.

"Who do you belong to?"

"You?"

"Is that a question, Beth? Before I give you an orgasm, you better know the man you're with."

"You, it's you, Knuckles."

"Once I put my dick inside you, there's no backing out. If I get too much, you'll tell me to stop. That's all I need. I don't need pretty words. I understand no, stop, don't."

"Yes, Knuckles."

"I also don't require you to call me Sir or Master."

"You don't sound like a Dom."

"Many men take what they want from the lifestyle and make it suit them. The leather you'll see me wear is that of my cut. Names, I'd rather know the woman that I want knows who is about to fuck her. Spread your pussy lips."

She did as he asked without hesitating, and he saw how wet she was, and he wanted to fuck her, so much. He kept his fingers inside her, working her pretty cunt.

He slid his tongue against her pussy, enjoying the taste of her some more. The instant he touched her clit, her pussy tightened around his fingers, and he couldn't help but moan. She was so incredibly tight. He'd never known a woman be so tight. Technically, she was still a virgin. She'd never willingly been with a man, and he intended for her first time with him to be perfect.

Knuckles wasn't in a rush to stick his dick inside her. One of the benefits of training to be a Dom, which he had done, he learned a great deal of restraint and patience at a time in his life when he'd needed it most. Being a Dom had taught him so many lessons, and if it hadn't been for the training, he truly believed he'd have ended up in serious trouble, not only with the law but with someone much worse. He wasn't a traditional Dom, and didn't need a harem of submissive women. Knuckles enjoyed the art of it, the mastery, and the trust. Until Beth trusted him completely, he could wait to explore more. Learning those skills allowed him to actually become a better man, and also a better brother. Where some of the club brothers would lash out, and inflict all kinds of pain, he wasn't like that. He liked to wait. Over time, Knuckles had learned the value of waiting. Patience brought out the innocence or the guilt in people. More people cracked under silence than anyone else, at least to him they had.

"You ever had this pretty pussy sucked?" he asked.

She shook her head.

"I'm going to be doing a lot of sucking of this, baby. You're just too damn perfect not to lick, suck, or fuck."

"I want you to fuck me, Knuckles."

"Not yet."

She groaned. "Why not?"

"You're not ready."

"I'm here, panting after you, begging for you to give it to me. I want you. I don't know how many more times I can prove to you that I do."

Knuckles removed his fingers and licked them clean. "Baby, I won't have you speaking to me like that. We talked about this, about who I am."

"I know who you are."

"Then you know I punish insolence, and I also punish spoiled little brats. Don't become a spoiled brat."

She groaned. "I don't mean to be."

"Tell me, Beth, has anyone ever given your pretty ass a spanking?"

"No one's ever called my ass pretty before."

He stood up and sat down on the sofa beside him. Wrapping his hands around her waist, he pulled her across him, and started to caress the curve of her ass. "It's so pretty, and full, and," he gave it a slap, "smackable."

"That's not a word."

"Oh, well, it's true. Your ass is just begging for a hand, baby."

He ran his fingers over the soft rounded curves, and then he spread her open, seeing the tight puckered hole of her anus.

"I've always been good. No one would dare hit me."

"Oh, Beth, there are ways to make you enjoy it so much more." He released her ass and brought his hand down on her plump flesh.

She gasped out.

He landed another blow on the cheek further away from him. Knuckles made sure not to be too hard on her. Beth might think she was ready for everything full on with him, but he wasn't a fool. She thought she was ready, and he was going to build her up to the man that he was. He was the man in charge, not her. Knuckles wouldn't be taking orders from her, or from anyone.

****

Beth's ass was nice and warm. Knuckles caressed her, and then hit her again, making her gasp. The touch was so light, yet it held a sting to it. Even as he spanked her, she couldn't help growing even more aroused. His cock pressed against her stomach, making her aware of how much he was enjoying her being close.

She closed her eyes, trying to make sense of everything that was happening to her, and she couldn't figure it out, not for a single second understand it.

"Damn," he said, squeezing her ass. "You've got the nicest ass I've seen. It's going to look so red and hot when I get my paddle to it."

Biting her lip, Beth for a second wondered if she'd bitten off more than she could chew. Knuckles was a red-blooded animal. A man who knew his own desires, and his own needs. She ... she didn't have the first clue about what she wanted.

She'd always put everything off, waiting for a different time. Denying herself sex, in place of fun. Going to parties, she'd thought that had made a difference to who she was.

Beth had believed parties made her fun, so it made people see her as fun.

It hadn't.

A life without the parties was simply a normal life.

She thought about her best friend, Maria, who was now married and had a child. Daisy and Maria were happily married, while Beth worked for a lawyer, arranging his clients, and she lived alone. Even Knuckles had tried to get her a cat. Did she look that miserable?

Knuckles slapped her ass, and in that one touch, fire ignited inside her.

The only person who had really helped her to feel was the man she was currently lying across. He showed her fire, passion, love, respect. Knuckles showed it all, and yet he even made sure she took some for herself.

Traveling this path with Knuckles would make her have to face herself, her own internal demons. There was no way he'd ever let her hide. She had to be willing to take on everything, and trust in him to never let her go, or to never break her.

This was not a decision to be taken lightly. She had to be ready to explore every part of herself, and to trust in Knuckles in ways she'd never trusted before.

Biting her lip, she had to wonder if she was capable of that.

Why not?

You're the reason you're here now.

"I can feel you thinking all the way up here, baby," he said. "I hope you come to the right decision."

"What would be the right decision?" she asked, hoping that he'd make it for her.

He leaned over her so that his lips were against her ear. "The decision that is right for you."

She groaned. Knuckles knew the game she was playing, and he had one of his own. He wasn't about to influence her decision either.

Knuckles slapped her ass twice, and then rubbed the area to soften her.

What do I have to lose?

Beth thought about the last few months of being near Knuckles. She'd always been near him but never dared to touch. When some of the club whores had gone to him, wrapping their arms around his neck, she'd been filled with jealousy. She didn't believe it was fair that they could touch him, and she couldn't.

"I want you," she said, coming to a decision.

This wasn't just tonight either.

She'd been thinking about this for a long time, much longer than when she moved in here. Beth had been thinking about it since the moment she saw him, the way he looked at her. When Knuckles was near, he made her feel safe, and alive. She wanted to keep on experiencing that, and the only way for that to ever happen, was for her to continue to be with him.

"You do?"

"Yes. I don't want to share you though." She glanced over her shoulder to look at him. "I want to be with you, and only be with you."

"I'm in charge, Beth, you know that."

"You didn't say if you're happy with being faithful."

He sighed, and she wondered if she'd fucked it up already.

"Beth, ever since you've come to the club, I haven't been with another female. It's not a question I need to answer because there's no one else I want but you." He lifted her up, and settled her down between his thighs, cupping her face as he did. "This has to involve total honesty between us. I need to know when I'm pushing too far, and you need to tell me when I'm not pushing you enough. I expect you to tell me at all times."

"Okay."

"Do you completely understand?"

"Yes, I do."

"Good." Suddenly he lifted her back up, and moved her to straddle his thighs. His hand sank into her hair, and he slammed his lips down on hers. She cupped his face, kissing him back with a ferocity that shocked her.

Beth held on tightly, loving the way his arms wrapped around her, holding her close.

His hands moved everywhere, running up and down her naked body.

Reaching between them, she wrapped her fingers around his cock, and started to work from the base up.

He groaned. "I've wanted your hands on me since the first day I saw you. You're fucking fire, Beth. No one can take that away from you."

Beth gasped as he moved her so that she was lying on the sofa. Knuckles took possession of her lips, sliding his tongue into her mouth, making her moan even more. He didn't stay for long. Kissing down her body, he paused at her breasts.

He pressed them together, licking the valley between, and sliding across each nipple. "Perfection."

After he sucked on each nipple, he moved down her body until he was poised over her pussy.

She watched as he opened the lips of her sex and sucked on her clit. She couldn't watch him for much longer than a few seconds. The pleasure was instant, and when he used his teeth, it made it even more exhilarating. She wanted that burst of pain combined with her pleasure.

Two fingers thrust inside her, going to the hilt, making her yearn for more.

"Baby, you're going to drive me crazy. I'm not going to know if I should be licking your pussy, or fucking it. Your body was made for me, and for me alone."

That, she truly believed.

He flicked his tongue across her clit, sliding down to fuck her. She groaned. Beth had been so close to another orgasm.

Knuckles drove her crazy, with an expert touch, driving her to the peak, holding her there, and then taking it away.

She screamed his name, begged for him to give her release, and he held it back.

"You'll come when I say you can come."

Beth stopped her begging, and basked in the pleasure his touch was providing. She'd never been explored, and Knuckles was savoring her body.

He stroked her pussy, licked, sucked, nibbled, and drew out every possible arousal from her.

"Come for me, Beth. Let me hear you come."

With the flick of his tongue, Beth erupted, coming so hard, and so deep, that she completely forgot who she was. The sensation made her feel like she was floating, and she closed her eyes, finally realizing after all this time what all the fuss was about.

Knuckles kept her there, stroking every last part of her orgasm out, until she finally couldn't stand anymore, and he brought her down gently.

When she opened her eyes, she saw Knuckles had his hand wrapped around his cock, the same hand that he'd used on her pussy. She saw her cream coating his dick.

She kept her legs open, but she couldn't look away from how he was touching his shaft. He seemed to be squeezing himself so tightly, almost as if he was hurting himself, yet Knuckles didn't seem hurt.

He worked his cock over and over, staring at her body.

"Fuck, baby, I don't know what it is you do to me."

Beth lay mesmerized as she watched Knuckles come, the white strands of his cum covering her stomach.

When he finished, and she was covered in his cum, he lay against her. She wrapped her arms around him, knowing it was one of the best experiences of her life, and she never wanted it to end.

"There's no going back now."

"I don't want to go back." She was looking forward to moving forward.

Chapter Six

A few days later

"How is it coming on the princess's car?" Brass asked.

Looking up from under the hood, Knuckles stared at him. "You're asking me that? I'm working on it."

"It has been over a week."

"So? We were waiting a week for the parts. I can't make this rush any more than I already have. She's getting shitty parts for it as it is."

Eliza didn't want the expense of buying brand new shit. So far, Knuckles had to send three parts back, and recalibrate some himself. He wasn't going to tire himself out on a bag of shit that was used to transport an entitled princess.

"Sorry, she's back in the reception," Brass said.

"Why are you talking like a fucking Prospect? You're a club brother. Tell her she's got to wait."

"I can't do that."

"Why?"

"I like her."

Knuckles sighed, wiping his hands on the cloth. "We have enough club pussy to keep you busy at the clubhouse. Why this woman?"

"I don't know. She's a princess, and I always wanted to deflower one of those, on my terms."

"So, you're going for the whole sympathy thing with looking like a pampered princess yourself?" Knuckles didn't have time for this shit. Duke wanted to bring the drug run forward, and the gun run that was usually spread out. He hated these runs, especially when his relationship with Beth was improving.

She understood he had a role to play in the club. He just didn't want her to think the club would come before her.

Fuck, he really didn't know what would come first.

Beth had gotten under his skin, and he couldn't leave her, not now.

"Look, I'll do anything you say. I mean it. I'll do whatever the hell you want."

"There's nothing you can give me."

Brass growled. Out of all of the brothers Brass was the most selfish. Dealing with him was like dealing with the fucking devil. The biggest problem, Brass was one of the most loyal brothers within the club. Trojans were inside him, and Knuckles wouldn't be without him, not ever. He was a pain in the ass, but he was a necessary pain in the ass.

"You know what. I've got a way to handle this." Knuckles moved past him, entering the reception area.

"Eliza Bishop, your piece of shit car isn't going to be ready for a while. The reason being, you want me to fix the piece of shit, while not causing any trouble yourself. Guess what, it's not going to happen. This car is staying with me until I can get it on the road, safe, and without a threat to yourself or to others. Now, if you have a problem, call your father, and let him come and get you. If not, Brass here wants to test drive your pussy, meaning he wants to fuck you into next week. If you've got a little rebellion inside you, give him a ride, and maybe he'll stop riding me."

"Wow, I, um, I came to bring lunch," Beth said.

During his rant, Knuckles hadn't seen his own woman, holding a brown baggy. "Now if you'll excuse me. I've got my own woman to attend to." Ducking under the counter, he rushed toward her, wrapping her up in his arms, and holding her close. "Fuck, baby, I missed you," he said.

He cupped her face, kissing her lips, sliding his tongue inside when she gasped, allowing him entry.

"Do I even want to know what was going on there?"

"Brass wants to fuck her."

"I did wonder why his tongue was dangling out, panting. I wonder if she'll fall for the act."

"You didn't?"

"I'm with you, aren't I? He was nice, kind of sweet, but I don't know, there was always an edge of lies to him. I'm not into that. I talked to Daisy about it once, and he said that Brass has many faults, but when he needed him, he was all right."

"He is. It's why we keep him around. Many clubs have them. You know, that one guy that's a total asshole, and you wonder why you haven't ended his sorry-ass existence." He reached down to cup her ass. "Anyway, what brought you here?"

"Well, I thought it would be nice for us to have lunch together, and also, I figured why the hell not. We're dating, aren't we?"

"That we are," he said, chuckling.

"Dating couples have lunch. If you feel I'm smothering you with my presence let me know."

"There's no smothering." Knuckles looked around the dirty yard, and shook his head. "Come on, there's a little park a few feet from here. We can sit under a tree."

He took hold of her hand, and they walked down the small stretch of road. Knuckles liked it. They weren't hiding who they were. Daisy had issues. The way he saw it, Daisy was her brother, so he had a right to act like an asshole. He didn't agree with it, but he wasn't about to start fighting with him.

"How was work?" Knuckles asked.

"Good. Clinton's got something going on. I don't know what. At first I thought it had to do with this woman he wants to date. He says it's not, and that the woman wouldn't return his calls. Usually he's the one dealing with the guys that have done wrong, or the guys in a divorce, or what not. He's gone to see a victim today. He didn't want me to come with him, and I haven't been allowed access to the file. It's kind of strange," she said.

He heard the concern in her voice, and he didn't like it. "Do you want me to go and talk to him?"

"No."

"Clinton will talk to me."

"I'm not having my boyfriend go and intimidate my boss. I can handle it. Clinton has always been a little weird anyway, no problem."

They entered the park, and he saw the children playing. He also saw Crazy with Leanna, and their little boy, Luke. Strawberry was in school.

"Let's go and say hi."

They walked up toward the happy couple.

"Well, well, well, does Daisy know?" Crazy asked.

Leanna tapped his arm. "Seriously, that's the first thing you're going to say to them?"

"It's not the only thing I'm going to say. God, woman, you don't need to hit so hard." Crazy gasped.

Beth laughed. "Daisy knows, and he's a little pissed about it, but then, he's only my brother, so it shouldn't matter what he says, should it?"

"Mommy, Daddy, look, look," Luke said, grabbing a pole, and sliding down it.

Knuckles chuckled. Crazy and Leanna hadn't

been around the club all that much in the last few months. They'd been doing some house changes, and getting Strawberry settled into a new school, which was closer to them.

Beth squeezed his hand and stood talking with Leanna.

"Is this going to cause some club trouble?"

"It shouldn't. Daisy knows I'm not messing around. It's the real deal."

"You going to claim her?"

"Yeah, I am. What about you? You and Leanna coming to give us a visit?"

"Soon. Shit with Strawberry has been a nightmare. Luke's been struggling as well." Crazy ran a hand down his face.

"What's wrong with Strawberry?" Knuckles asked.

"Fucking childhood bullies is what. Fucking sick of them."

"Seriously? Your kid is getting bullied? How the fuck does that work?" From what Knuckles knew, none of them had ever gotten bullied throughout high school. In fact, even Matthew had been left alone, and he'd gone through many years a scrawny kid.

"None of the kids believe her that her father's part of the Trojans. They upset her because of her name, and shit. Kid stuff."

"I'd say go and pick her up, take a few of the guys with you. No one bullies Strawberry and gets away with it."

"I'm not about to scare the shit out of a bunch of kids."

"I'm not saying we get out and threaten them. I think a show of force, let them know who Strawberry comes from. It's a visual thing."

"She's nearly eight years old."

"They're only going to get bigger. Nip it in the bud now. Don't let it go crazy. Anyway, I've got a lunch to enjoy." He wrapped his arm around Beth, and lifted her up. "Sorry we can't stay to chat."

"Bye, Leanna, we'll talk soon."

****

"I can't believe you did that," Beth said, handing him his meal, which she'd gotten from the diner.

"What? If I left you talking with Leanna, I wouldn't have been able to see you."

Beth had been worried that it was a dumb ass idea to bring him food. Now, she was really pleased that she had. "Brass wants to screw that woman in the shop?"

"Yeah. She's an entitled princess, and I'm having to fix her car."

"Do you like working with cars?"

"It's something I've always been able to do. I love being part of the club, and I've got jobs to do there as well."

She took out the plastic fork for her chicken Cobb salad, and took a bite, staring at Knuckles. He was loving the burger she got him, with extra bacon.

"I heard you guys were going on another run?" she asked. Maria had called her up, and they'd gotten talking, her friend letting it slip that Daisy was leaving in a few weeks.

"Yeah, one next week, and one at the end of this week. It has been brought forward. I'll be in touch constantly."

"Is it dangerous?"

Knuckles paused, staring at her. "Do you trust me?"

"Yes."

"Then trust me when I say to you that I will make

it back to you."

She licked her lips. "I can't stop thinking about our night together."

"Me neither, babe. I'm sorry I haven't been around. With the ride coming forward, I've had to check over the bikes. Raoul has been helping me. Time has gotten away."

She touched his arm. "I'm not complaining, not really. It's just, I worry about you, Knuckles. I do. This is going to be the first time that a ride like this is going to mean anything to me, and I find that a little scary. Will you be coming over tonight?"

"Yeah, I will. How about I pick you up from work?"

She shook her head. "I could cook us some dinner, if you'd like. My treat." She could also put that sheer negligee to good use and tempt him with something a little more.

"Okay. When I'm done here, I've got to head back to the clubhouse, and then I'll be with you. What do you think?" Knuckles asked.

"I love it."

Glancing behind her, she saw they were in a secluded part of the park. No one could see them. Putting her carton onto the ground, she moved up his body, straddling his legs.

"Now, what do I owe the pleasure of this, baby?"

"This is letting you know that I miss you." She wrapped her arms around his neck, pressing her lips to his. Beth kissed down his neck, to his ear. "I've been touching myself the past couple of days, missing you. I miss you so much, Knuckles."

"Fuck. Have you come?"

"Sometimes. I'm not as good as your wicked tongue. I think about you, Knuckles."

He wrapped his burger up and sank his fingers into her hair, wrapping the length around his knuckles. She couldn't help but smile, thinking about his name, and what he was doing.

"It would seem to me, sweet Beth, you want to be punished."

"No."

Did she want to be punished?

"You're not allowed to touch yourself again until I say so."

"But I get so wet, and late at night after I've woken up from a dream, I can't help it."

"You dream about me?"

"Yes."

"In this dream, what am I doing?"

"You're touching me."

"Anything else?"

"You're making me watch as you touch me. It's so damn hot, and you're always in charge, Knuckles, always. You're the master of me."

"Always, baby. Now, we're going to have to head back to the shop. I don't want to risk damaging kids' eyes for what I want to do to you."

She shivered with delight. Gathering up the remains of her food, she took Knuckles hand, and they rushed back to the mechanic shop. She was surprised to see Duke and Brass working. Knuckles didn't stop until they were back in the private office. She saw the blinds had already been drawn. He pushed her up against the door, grabbing her hands, and slamming them above her head.

"Now, it seems to me you think you can do whatever the hell you want without consequences for your actions?"

She shook her head. "No, that's not what I think."

Beth wasn't afraid. She was so turned on, she didn't know how she was able to form coherent words. He was driving her crazy.

"Silence. We're going to have some new rules. When you're alone with me in private, you don't talk other than to say if I'm going too far, understand? Don't be a smartass either. Know that I mean it when we're like this, on the verge of fucking each other."

Suddenly, he spun her around so that her face was to the door. He shoved her hands above her head, and his hand moved to her stomach. Knuckles pressed against her back, and she moaned, feeling the rock hard ridge of his dick pressing against her ass.

"Keep your hands there. Don't move them."

He released her hands and slapped her ass. The action startled her.

"How many times have you played with yourself?" he asked.

"Six times."

Knuckles slapped her ass again. "Your pussy belongs to me. How many times have I slapped your ass?"

"Twice."

"Good. Count them."

She counted each blow, which got harder, and stung a little deeper. The heat from the punishment made her even wetter. She wanted him so badly.

"Six," she said, on the final spank, and she was a little gutted that it was over.

"Now, that is what I call a good punishment, baby." The hand on her stomach moved down into her pants. "Let's see how much you enjoyed my punishment."

She opened her legs, and he touched her naked slit.

Her cheeks heated as she felt how wet she was. She'd never been this wet before in her life, and now, Knuckles knew.

"Do you know how badly I want to slam my dick inside you right now? It would be so easy to release my cock, and sink into your wet cunt." He nibbled her neck.

"There's nothing to stop you," she said.

"Yes, there is. The first time I'm with you, it's not going to be against the door. I'm going to have time to explore your body, and get you even hotter for me."

He slid two fingers inside her, and she tried to press down on his fingers, to make him go deeper within her.

"It's not enough," she said, moaning.

"When my dick is inside you, you'll be screaming about how there's too much."

He brought his fingers up, to stroke over her clit.

Knuckles pinched the bud, and then soothed out the sting with his fingers. "When I say you can come, you come."

Beth nodded, unable to deny him.

He fingered her pussy, teasing her. "Come for me."

She shattered around his fingers. Only Knuckles's hold on her kept her upright. Six times she'd brought herself to orgasm. Six times it had been good but not amazing. Beth would never touch herself until Knuckles gave her permission. She wanted what he was giving her.

Knuckles continued to finger her until every last bit of pleasure eased up, and then he pulled his fingers from her, licking her cream.

"I look forward to tonight."

"Me too," she said.

He spun her back around and slammed his lips down on hers. She followed his lips as he pulled away from the kiss. "Come on, I'm going to walk you back to Clinton's."

"You don't have to do that. I can make my way there."

"It will be my pleasure." He grabbed his leather jacket, and she walked with him back to Clinton's. Her body felt like it was on cloud nine. At the door to her office, he claimed another kiss, and he waited until she was inside before leaving. The moment he was gone, she rushed into the bathroom, locked the door, and shoved her skirt up over her ass. Dropping her panties, she stared in the mirror at her red ass. Knuckles had done that, and she'd loved it.

Running her fingers over the cheeks, she smiled.

She belonged to Knuckles, and it was this way where he marked her that affirmed it to her.

Licking her lips, she brushed up her lipstick and put her clothing back into place. Beth felt new, reborn, and confident. Entering the main office, she saw that Clinton was reading through a file.

"How did it go with your latest client?" she asked.

"Interesting actually. Hold my calls. I'm going to be busy." He looked up and frowned.

She offered him a smile, and took a seat at her desk. "Is something wrong, Mr. Briars?"

"Not at all. I'm just wondering if I'm missing something."

"Not that I know of."

"Huh," he said, and walked into his office. She looked forward to tonight.

Chapter Seven

"What do you mean he just walked away and left?" Holly asked, standing by her stove with a hand on her hip.

Mary shrugged. "He hasn't been back since. I couldn't bring myself to go to the clubhouse."

"This is all about Mac, and the fact you're working with him?"

"Yeah, he asked me how I'd feel if he was around Lori, Lilah, and Emma." Mary buried her head into her hands, sobbing.

"Sweetie, don't cry." Holly rushed to her side, pulling her into a hug. They had been friends for as long as she could remember. This was so embarrassing for Mary. She'd avoided Holly over the past couple of days. What woman wanted to admit that their husband had walked out?

"Starlight has been asking where he is. He hasn't even called, and I don't know what to do, or what to say." She once again covered her face. "I hate this."

"Tell me from the beginning exactly what happened," Holly said, taking a seat at the table in the kitchen.

Mary told her about their arguments, and how Pike wanted her to end things with Mac, even though there was nothing going on, and she couldn't believe for a second that he'd even think that, and yet he was.

She felt so broken.

"Sweetie, as much as I hate to say this, maybe you do need to see it from his perspective."

"What do you mean?"

Before Holly could say anything, the door opened, and seconds later, Duke entered, with Drake by his side, holding his hand. "Perfect. Duke, baby, if I was to start up a business with Raoul, how would that make you feel?"

Mary gasped. Raoul and Holly had some history between them. Their history being, Raoul had taken Holly to prom, taken her virginity, and proceeded to tell everyone at the club about it. It had been a mortifying moment for Holly, and Mary recalled the time she'd been crying.

"It wouldn't happen. You'll do business with me. Don't get me wrong, my shit with Raoul was settled, but I'd have to start questioning you and what you're trying to do." Duke looked at Holly, then at her. "What's this about?"

"It's different. You slept with Raoul. I never have with Mac."

"Ah, that explains why Pike's sulking like a fucking baby. What's gotten into you two?" Duke asked.

"Pike left me."

Duke looked shocked. "He left you?"

"Yep. He walked away three nights ago, and he hasn't been back since."

"Fuck! That explains the drinking, and the crap that is going on with him. Babe, you take Drake. I'm going to go and see Pike."

"Why?" Mary asked.

"He may be a club brother, but there's a reason he's my VP. I trust him, and he's my friend. This shit you got going down with Mac, it's not fair to him, or to Mac."

"It's for the blog."

"Screw the fucking blog, Mary. You've got more than enough people to fucking experiment on. You don't see Holly going around chasing for that shit." Duke shook his head. "You know what, it would probably do for you to see him with another woman before you finally got your head out of your ass, and see what the fuck you're doing." Duke slammed out of the door.

"Daddy said a bad word," Drake said.

Mary felt the tears and hated herself. She looked over at Holly to see her friend looking uncomfortable.

"What?" Mary asked.

"He's right, Mary. You're my best friend, and you know I love you. Duke's right about this. I did think it was a little weird that you kept on at the diner, and I did think you were keeping Mac as a backup in case things went sour with Pike." Holly shrugged. "Then you had Starlight, and you were both so happy, but I've even noticed you're spending more and more time with Mac."

"There's nothing going on."

"*Now*, no, there's not. Tell me, Mary, when things started to get bad between you and Pike, did you cut your hours back?"

"No. Why should I?"

"I think it would be best for you to sit down, and think about what you want. You're giving two men mixed messages, and I don't feel comfortable being in the middle with that. I love you, and I'll be here."

"The blog, Holly."

"The blog is doing better than either of us could imagine. Vale Valley has enough picnics and local events that we can save all of our testing for then. Trying out the food at the diner was great, and it was fun, but Mac has remained single. I've never even seen him into a woman. I don't think you're being fair to either man. I'm sorry."

Just like that, Mary saw the problem, but she didn't know how to solve it.

****

Pike stared down into the beer bottle and found that another was indeed empty. Someone was drinking all of his beer, and he snorted. Yep, *he* was drinking all of his beer, and he didn't give a shit. Fuck what he was supposed to do? It was drinking time somewhere in the world, and he was going to have a blast.

Another day, same problems, and one solution, drink.

Landon dropped down into a seat beside him, and Pike released a burp. "Tell you what, kid, don't ever get married. It's a fucking waste, and believe me, they only drain you of everything."

"What the hell?" Landon asked.

"Just telling it like it is."

"What the fuck is this man talking about?" Landon asked, looking toward the barman.

"I don't know. He's spent the past few days drinking."

"Maybe he needs some company," Lori said, coming up toward him. She ran her hand down his back, and he growled, then paused. Mary had been his whole life for so long that he'd gotten what it was all about being with another woman.

No, he didn't want to fuck away his troubles. Mary was his whole world, and he wasn't about to fuck another woman and risk his marriage. Yeah, his marriage was in the fucking toilet, but he wasn't about to drown it.

"Get the fuck off me, skanky bitch." He shoved her away.

"So, you're drinking then," Duke said, drawing his attention. Rolling around, he stared at his friend. In that moment Duke was not his Prez. They were friends.

"Drinking is the one thing that I can do right. I don't see why I should give it up." He raised his beer bottle, only to find that it was still empty. "Prospect, another."

Duke took a seat at the bar. "I heard what

happened. You left?"

"Yeah, I left. She wouldn't listen to the shit I had to say. Her and fucking Mac. Bastard owns a diner, and she picked me. We've got a kid together. Fucking Miss Star. Miss Mary too. Everything is totally fucked."

"What the fuck is going on?" Landon asked.

"Pike left Mary."

"Fuck, for real?"

"For fucking real!" Pike took a swallow of the beer, and released another belch. "We're undecided right now. Mary doesn't think I know what I'm talking about. I know what I see in the way Mac looks at her. Mac and Mary." Just saying the two names together angered Pike. "I shouldn't have let her continue on at the diner."

"You thought Mac would move on."

"He hasn't. Fucker is probably pining for my woman, and I can't do fuck-all about it."

Duke knocked on the bar. "Drink, I want one."

"You're going to drink this early with me?"

"Don't have much of a choice. I'm not going to let you drink on your own. So I will drink with you."

"That's rather sweet," Pike said. He turned to Landon. "You drinking?"

"Sure."

That's what he needed. A day of drinking and laughter to push the pain away. Even as he thought it, Pike knew it wasn't what he needed. What he needed was back at home, determined to break his heart.

****

Knuckles stood outside of Beth's apartment and ran his fingers through his hair. He had just escaped a drinking party from hell. There was no way he was going to get caught up in Pike and Mary's problems.

When he'd gotten to the clubhouse, he'd seen that several of the brothers were already drunk off their asses.

He'd rushed to his room to change. On the way out, he'd avoided them and gotten out of the way.

Knocking, he waited for Beth to answer.

When she did, words were taken right out of his mouth. She wore a stunning, figure hugging black dress that went to her knee. Her hair was in curls, and she looked mouth-watering.

"Hey, you're a little late. I was worried you weren't going to come."

"I had to run and hide. Pike's getting over his issues with Mary by drinking them."

"Maria told me they were having troubles. I don't know why, just that they are."

"I didn't stay to linger."

He entered the apartment and stared at her. "Are you wearing panties?" he asked.

She shook her head. "No."

"Have you touched yourself?"

"No."

Knuckles saw she told the truth.

"Well, you've been a good girl, so I guess it's only fair that we have dinner."

"Actually," she said. "Dinner is in the fridge. It's a salad. I was going to make you an elaborate dinner, and then, I decided, salad would work best."

"Why did you think that?" he asked.

She sank to her knees before him, resting her palms on her thighs. Beth raised her head up, and he was completely lost with her.

"I wanted to give you the same pleasure that you'd given me."

She pushed her dress down her arms until it fell beneath her naked breasts. This side of Beth he hadn't expected, but he was loving it. Knuckles loved how she was growing in confidence when she was around him, and also, taking what she wanted, without fear.

Beth reached for his zipper, and he didn't stop her as she dragged it down. He stayed still, letting her do all the work, and for her to push her own kind of boundaries. She peeled his jeans away and pushed them down to his ankles.

His cock sprang forward as he rarely, if ever, wore underwear. He didn't like the constricting fabric against his dick.

She touched his shaft, wrapping her fingers around the base. He watched, mesmerized as she worked up and down his length, starting out slow, and building up to a steady pace. Knuckles told her when to hold him a little tighter, and guided her in touching him. He didn't like too much pain, nor did he like too little.

If she was touching him, he wanted to actually feel it.

"I want to taste you, Knuckles."

This woman was a dream come true. He wanted her to as well.

She moved up and slicked her tongue against the tip, flicking her tongue backward and forward, licking up his pre-cum. Only when she was ready, did she cover the whole head of his dick and take him into her mouth. She sucked a few inches, and pulled away, looking up at him.

"Am I doing it right?"

"Yeah, baby, you're doing it really well," he said.

Beth covered his dick once again, and he stroked her hair, gripping the length, and showing her how he liked it. He thrust into her mouth to the point that she started to gag. When it was too much, he pulled out of her mouth, giving her the chance to grow accustomed to it again.

"You've got such a pretty mouth, baby. Such a pretty mouth," he said.

He pumped into her mouth, knowing he wasn't going to last. The only time he'd been reaching orgasm was when he was with her. Their time together meant so much to him that he hadn't wanted to pressure her.

Now, he saw he wasn't pressuring her, and to a point, Beth was taking the lead in their relationship with him bringing guidance to her.

"I want you," she said, releasing his cock long enough to say.

"You're going to have me."

He'd been hoping to hold out for longer, but he saw the error of his ways. He and Beth had been dancing around this for a long time, and now the time for waiting was over.

Tugging on her hair, he forced her to release him, and he beat the seed from his cock, splashing her naked tits as he did so.

Once his orgasm ended, he sank to his knees, cupped her face, and kissed her.

"Don't say no, please don't say no. I'm ready, Knuckles. I want to belong to you, no one else."

"Baby, I'm not going to deny you. What just happened, I'm not going home from. I'm going to make you mine, completely."

****

Mary entered the diner and saw Mac at one of the tables, scribbling notes down, and probably orders for the upcoming weekly meals she had planned. It was closed tonight as they had advertised a half day. This was usually the night she spent with Pike. Holly would take Starlight, and they would have a night for themselves.

"Hello," she said.

Mac spun around, looking startled.

"I'm sorry, I didn't meant to scare you."

"It's me. I was lost in figures and shit. Come in,

by all means come in. You own half of the diner anyway. I thought you'd be with Pike. I know this is your date night."

She took a seat and stared at him. Mac was a handsome man, and if Pike hadn't been the one she fell in love with first, she'd have probably fallen for Mac.

"I'm sure you've heard that Pike has left me," she said.

"Wait? What? No, I haven't heard that." Mac put down his pen. "I'm so sorry." He reached over and touched her hand. She stared at the touch of his hand, and she hated that fact that all she saw was friendship whereas everyone else saw more. She loved Pike, and Mac had never stood a chance.

"Do you love me?" she asked.

Never in all of her life did she think she'd have to confront a man about his feelings.

"What?" Mac asked.

"It's a simple question. I know you wanted something more from me, and that I'm good for the diner. Do you care for, love, want me?" she asked.

He released her arm, looking uncomfortable. "Mary?"

"No, I need to know, because right now, my little girl is staying with my friend while I'm here. She hasn't seen her father, and I've had my friend tell me something isn't right between the two of us. You're one of my friends, Mac. Tell me what you feel."

"Look, I'm really sorry—"

"Goddamn it, Mac, just answer my question. Are you my friend or not?"

He sighed. "I'm not."

Mary stared at him in shock. She had believed he would laugh at what Holly, Duke, and Pike were saying. Instead, this was all her fault, and she saw it now. She owed Pike more than an apology.

"Excuse me?"

"Come on, Mary. At first I pretended I didn't. You've made this place shine in ways I never could. That blog of yours, I saw how much it meant, and I figured this would be a safe haven for you." He shrugged.

"I'm with Pike."

"Yet he rarely comes here anymore. I figured things were rough with you."

"I never knew."

"Never knew what? That someone could have a crush, fall in love, want you? Mary, you're a beautiful woman. Your food is amazing, you're amazing. After all this time, you didn't have a clue? An inkling?"

"No. I thought if you had women that I'd never seen it was because you wanted it to remain private."

"There hasn't been anyone, and there won't be anyone."

Mary shook her head. "I'm sorry, Mac. I'm in love with Pike, and I only ever saw you as a friend." She reached into her purse. "You once gave me half the business, and now I'm giving it back."

"Mary?"

"No, don't Mary me, or anything. This is what has to happen. I care about you, Mac, I do. I'll never, ever, ever be in love with you. This is my fault. I thought it was possible to be friends with someone, and that was the lie. I'm so fucking stupid." Mary placed the documents on the table and left the diner.

"I do love you, Mary. I'll treat you better than Pike, and I'd always treat Starlight like my own."

She closed her eyes and turned to look at him. How had she been so blind?

"Mac, she has a father, and it's not you. It's never going to be you. She loves her dad, Pike. He's her father." Throughout the whole of her life she had never wanted to hurt anyone, yet she had failed, and hurt the one man she loved the most. Even though in her heart she was telling herself to walk away, she turned back. This needed to be final so Mac had no doubt at all. "I love Pike. I'm in love with Pike. It has always been him, and it will always be him. I don't love you."

She left the diner with tears in her eyes.

Mac had been a friend. In her heart she had seen him as only a friend, and now she had learned that he thought he was something different.

Walking down the street, she saw that Sheila, Holly's mother, had waited for her. Russ, Holly's dad, had gone to the clubhouse to be with Pike, and Sheila had come to her.

"Are you okay, honey?" Sheila asked.

"Everything everyone else said was the truth. I was the one living the lie." She batted away her tears. "Pike's getting drunk?"

"Yes."

"Will you take me to the clubhouse in the morning?" Mary asked.

"Yes."

She had to salvage her marriage. Mary couldn't let it fall apart. She had already done enough damage as it was.

Chapter Eight

Knuckles picked Beth up and carried her through to the main bedroom. He was going to give her the night of her life, and he wasn't going to take no for an answer. She belonged to him, and they belonged together. He'd never been surer of anything else in his life than the way Beth felt to him.

"I can walk."

"I don't care." He pushed her to the bed and followed her down. Caressing her body, he moved between her thighs, opening her up. "You're mine, baby."

"I know."

"You'll always be mine. You know what that means?"

"Claiming me in front of the club."

"Your brother wouldn't be there to see it."

"Knuckles, you're naked between my legs. I don't want to be talking about Daisy."

He smirked. "Don't worry, you won't be thinking about him much longer." Kissing her neck, he started to trail his lips down to her nipples. He flicked each one, and moved to the next, devoting careful attention to each one. Gliding down her body, he paused at her navel, nibbling even more. Her stomach quivered, and he took his time, flicking out his tongue, and teasing her some more.

"Baby, you're so beautiful," he said.

This first time, he wanted her to be so overtaken by pleasure that any past experience she had would be completely annihilated.

Moving between her thighs, he opened her pussy lips and stared. She really was pretty, even her cunt.

He wanted a taste of her. Knuckles also liked his woman to look like one, so he didn't mind the small patch of pubic hair just above her lips. He saw she'd shaved away the rest from her lips. Flicking his tongue across her clit, he glided it down, going to her entrance. Pushing inside her, he moaned as more cream exploded on his tongue.

Fucking inside her, he got her even wetter before he moved back up to suck on her clit.

His cock already started to swell, and he wanted inside her.

Knuckles was determined to make her dripping wet. He wasn't small.

"Oh, God, that feels amazing."

Sucking her clit into his mouth, he flicked his tongue backward and forward. Pushing two fingers inside her, he started to fuck her, drawing out her orgasm, and getting her used to having him inside her.

Beth shattered around his fingers. Knuckles wasn't about to punish her. There were many parts to his dominance. He didn't require her to come on demand. Besides, tonight was a huge breakthrough for her, and he wasn't about to spoil what was happening by his words.

Removing his fingers from her pussy, he licked them, while looking up at her.

"I've got some condoms," he said.

"Me too." She reached toward her drawer and produced one. "I did have plans for this to happen the first night you cooked me dinner."

"How long have you been trying to get me into bed?"

"A while. It started at the club, but I saw you weren't convinced. I figured if I showed you I'd grown up, and gotten to be more me, you'd accept it."

"Baby, I've accepted that you're a big girl for a

long time." He took the condom from her, tearing into it, and sliding the latex over his dick.

She licked her lips, and he was reminded of how good her lips were to have around his cock. He ran his thumb across her lip, and she opened up, sucking on his thumb.

"What are you thinking about, Knuckles?" she asked.

"You've got no idea. I want you so damn bad."

Moving up the bed, he settled between her thighs. Knuckles wasn't in a rush for this to end, and he wanted her lips more than anything. Cupping her cheek, he took possession of her mouth, sliding his tongue inside.

"Taste yourself," he said. "You taste so good."

She licked his lips, moaning along with him.

Pulling away, he gripped the base of his cock and placed the tip to her entrance. Staring into her pretty blue eyes, he slowly started to work his cock inside her. Knuckles didn't look away. He kept his gaze on her, determined to see every reaction.

"You're big," she said, gasping.

"I know. Tell me if it's too much."

She shook her head. "It feels amazing."

"You feel amazing."

And she did. Her pussy was so tight, and hot. Knuckles pushed two inches inside her. When more of him was inside her, he moved his hands to rest beside his body. He made her look at him, by not looking away. Knuckles didn't want to miss a second of this, and he was determined for her to see who she belonged to.

There was no doubt in his mind that Beth would be his old lady. It was who she was supposed to be.

"Please," she said.

"I don't want to hurt you."

"I don't care. I want you all, Knuckles. No

holding back. I don't want to hold back, not from you."

He pushed another inch inside her, gritting his teeth against the pleasure. He was going to wait. Damn it, he was torn between giving her what she wanted, and doing what he knew was right. Her sweet words, and finally, her tightening pussy were too much.

Thrusting the entire length of his dick within her cunt, Knuckles paused at the hilt of her, even as she gave a gentle scream. He wasn't small. Even Lori had complained about how big he was.

Fuck, don't think about those women.

This is Beth, and they don't have a place right now.

This was about them, not other women.

Opening his eyes, he stared into hers, and he saw that satisfied smile.

"Wow," she said. "I'm not going to break, Knuckles."

She touched his waist, and that touch was like lightning, shocking him to the core. Beth had come into his world, and into his heart. He'd never been a sentimental kind of guy. This woman, she was making him be something he'd never even conceived.

Keeping himself still within her, he felt every single twitch of her pussy. She tightened around him, squeezing him like a fist, her cream making it easy for him to claim her.

"It doesn't have to hurt," she said.

"Baby, I'll never hurt you. Every time with me will be just as amazing." He'd make sure of it.

She smiled. "Who would have thought that my big, bad biker had feelings?"

Knuckles leaned down, capturing her lips. It wasn't enough. Sliding his tongue against the seam of her lips, he waited for her to let him inside. Tonight was all about the two of them exploring each other. Soon, they could explore an entirely different territory in their relationship. This was what they had been dancing around for nearly two years.

Plunging his tongue into her mouth, he started to rock within her.

Her pussy kept trying to make him go deeper, but he got her accustomed to the length and width of him. He went slowly at first until her cream started to gather, making it a much easier fit for him, so he glided within her with ease.

"Please, Knuckles. I can't wait. I need you. Please fuck me."

He wasn't one to let a woman go on waiting. Taking hold of her hands, he locked them above her head, and making her watch him, he pulled all of the way out of her.

"You're mine, Beth. No other man will know how sweet you taste, or how you sound. This is all going to be mine."

"I've been yours since I met you," she said.

"Baby, you've been mine since I first saw your picture." Slamming inside her, Knuckles fucked her hard, and Beth begged him for more. Driving inside her, he started to ride her hard, and when she was getting close to orgasm, he slowed down, making it almost painful with her need.

"Yes, yes, please."

Silencing her with his lips, he fucked her hard, giving and taking with equal measure. The bed banged against the wall.

"We come together," he said, voice hoarse.

"Yes."

Slamming inside her, he rode her, screaming for her to come, and she did at the same time as he did.

Filling up the condom, he was a little upset that it wasn't inside her, but that would come soon.

Staying within her walls, he rested beside her, stroking her cheek.

Tears filled her eyes, dripping down her cheeks. Knuckles didn't say anything as he knew she was dealing with her demons right about now.

"I've been afraid for so long," she said.

"You don't have to be afraid anymore. I've got you. I'll always have you."

"I never knew it could be like this. I was afraid."

"And now?"

"Now, I'm so glad you didn't give up on me, or walk away. I don't know what I'd have done if you walked away."

Knuckles smiled. "There's no chance of that. You need a fighter by your side, and you've got him in me. I'll fight all of your battles."

"Who will fight yours? I want to be that woman."

"Beth, you are that woman. You don't even realize how strong you are."

****

Sex had been amazing. Beth stared into Knuckles's dark eyes, and knew even before now that she loved him. She had loved him for a long time. Moving out of the clubhouse had been a hard decision to make, but it had been something she had to do to prove to herself that she was strong.

He pulled out of her, and she winced a little.

"I'm hungry," he said.

"I've got a salad to cover it."

Climbing off the bed, each little twinge made her smile and elate inside. She'd had sex, and it had been wonderful. Beth wanted to dance around the room, screaming for the victory that had just occurred. Instead, she glided serenely into her kitchen, and bent down, grabbing the large bowl of salad.

Placing it on the table, she got a couple of plates, and a few other things, buttering some bread.

Knuckles came out, completely naked, just like her. His cock was flaccid, but even so, he was a big man. Licking her lips, she recalled how he felt and tasted on her tongue. She wanted that again.

"This looks delicious."

"I spent some time in the kitchen with Holly and Mary. They do know what they're doing. I learned a few tricks from them."

"They have that magical way of drawing you in, don't they?"

"Tell me about it. I was only sitting there asking questions, and they were taking pictures. I never knew so much went into a blog."

"Both women take it totally seriously. It's about food, and they take food seriously. They don't like to think any of their recipes would fail. It's why you get so many tasting sessions. They make sure everything is perfect before letting the blog post go live." He took a seat, and grabbed a fork. She watched as he took a large bite, and moaned. "This is damn good."

"Yay, I'm so glad." She started eating her own, taking up a bun and biting into it. "Do you do anything for the blog? You talk about it enough?"

"No, I don't do anything, not really. Well, besides from being tasters for it, and they use me to experiment on."

"I can see that. You're good for experimenting." A lot more dirty things were running through her mind.

"Eat some food. You've got a long night, and we can experiment some more very soon."

She closed her thighs, trying to create a delightful

friction against her clit. Being around Knuckles aroused her. He set her on fire with need.

They finished their salad, and she listened as Knuckles talked about the latest car he was working on.

"That's the woman I saw today, right?"

"Yep. Brass wants to fuck her, and I'm bored with having to deal with him. She's a pampered princess making a show of rebellion."

"You don't like pampered princesses?"

"I don't like it when people tell me how to do my job."

"Rusty Frank tells you."

"The guy's ancient. He probably knows more about cars that I do."

"Yet he comes to the shop regularly to get his car fixed." She chuckled. "I imagine he likes testing you. Seeing how long it is before you tell him no more."

"It doesn't matter. I can understand why he loves that car. It has got a lot of memories. He even told me the back seat was where he made his first daughter." He laughed. "Of course, I know that I've changed the original back seating, if not someone else before I came along."

"That's what you like, memories?"

"Yeah, we've got to make them. I'd like to think that I can make some damn good memories."

"What was life like as a child?"

"I didn't have the kind of upbringing you or Daisy had."

"I didn't ask if you did."

"My parents put me in foster care when I was five years old. They decided they no longer wanted a kid. They wanted each other. I wish I could saw they were crack whores, but they weren't. Both were respectable, working people."

"Wow."

"Yeah, wow. I was too much of a handful for their organized lives." Knuckles shrugged.

Beth packed away their food and took a seat. "Did you get adopted?"

"A couple of times. I was always a loner, you know. I didn't need to be part of a crowd to be accepted. It's what makes being part of the Trojans a little different for me. I never ran with a crowd, or got into any trouble. For the most part, I was a boring kid. Kept my head down, studied, and didn't cause trouble." He smiled. "The foster homes where I was part of a large group, they didn't want to give me up, and to an extent they nurtured me."

"What happened?"

"I got a good education, and they made sure I was taken care of. They understood me. Once I graduated, I got a job, and I went to night-college. One of my jobs, I worked in a gym, where I happened to meet my first Mistress."

"Mistress?"

"A Domme."

"Okay," she said.

He laughed. "I wasn't a submissive, and they took me to a club, where I found other men with the same likes as myself. I didn't have the same needs as they did, but it helped to bring me focus. That's why I like the life, and that is why I trained as a Dom, and then one night, when I was about nineteen, twenty, I was in a bar where Russ was there. One thing led to another, and within a year, I was prospecting for the Trojans MC. I earned my patch, and I haven't looked back since."

"No family?"

"No family, no ties. I sometimes go to the foster home to see how everyone is, but other than that, nothing."

Beth tilted her head to the side, and smiled. Getting to her feet, she moved toward him, and Knuckles pulled away from the table. She straddled his waist, sinking her fingers into his hair and staring into his dark eyes. Most people talked about her own eyes, or lighter colors, blue, green, hazel. Not many people complimented dark eyes, and yet Knuckles' eyes, they were a glimpse into his soul. Access to him.

"I'd never give you up, or put some somewhere else. You're mine, Knuckles, just like I am yours."

Cupping his face, she took possession of his lips, and moaned as he cupped her ass, pulling her close. His once flaccid cock was rock hard, and pressing against her naked pussy.

"We need a condom," he said.

She climbed off him and went to grab a condom. Rushing back, she tore into the packet and pulled out the latex. Sinking to her knees, she held his length, and rolled the condom over his cock.

"Fuck, even you putting a condom on me feels so damn good."

She giggled. "I should try and do it more often."

"Hell yeah, I'm not going to complain."

Beth took the lead, holding his cock to her entrance, and slowly, seating herself on his length. She released a little gasp as he started to fill her.

He grabbed her hips, and slammed her completely down on his cock, making her cry out. Knuckles filled her to the brim, almost to the point of pain.

"Yes, baby, ride my cock."

Holding onto his shoulders, she started to ride his dick, moaning as he filled her. Pulling off him until only the tip was inside her, she slammed down to take more of him inside.

"Perfect, so fucking perfect."

"Yes, fuck me, Knuckles."

"Baby, you're the one doing all the fucking. I'm just along for the ride here."

He held her hips, and together they rocked to completion. It was short, amazing, and Beth shook with the power of her orgasm.

"You're going to be my old lady, even if I have to enter the ring with Daisy," he said.

She sat up, and stared at him. "You'd do that?"

"Of course I would. When are you going to realize that for you, sweet Beth, I'll do whatever it takes to make you mine?"

"I think I'm starting to realize that."

He trailed a hand down her back, and she sighed, wrapping her arms around him. Knuckles held her close, and she caressed his chest, loving the feel of him. "Daisy won't believe that you want me."

"Don't worry, I'll make him see."

Knuckles laughed. "The problem with Daisy, he doesn't always listen to reason."

Chapter Nine

Brass stared across town as Eliza walked between the shops. She'd just been in the accessory shop, and came out with a lovely looking handbag. It made him wonder where she was getting the money from. Then again, he wondered if she was even away from her parents or if she was pretending.

Sipping his coffee, he wondered what the hell he was doing here, watching her again. She stared through the windows, looking, and moving on. When she crossed the street, he waited for her to get close to him. Glasses covered her green eyes, and her raven hair was pulled into a ponytail on top of her head.

He stopped in front of her, and she gasped, looking up at him. "Brass?"

"Hey," he said.

She licked her lips, glancing all around them. Since Knuckles had let it out that he wanted to fuck her, she had disappeared out of the shop without saying a word.

"Um, how's my car?"

"It's still in the shop. How's shopping?"

"I caved with the bag. I really shouldn't have, but I got a job. I start tomorrow at Mac's diner. It's really quite nice. He was suddenly hiring this morning."

"Do you know how to serve?"

"I do, actually. I worked at a small restaurant when I was a kid." She lifted up her glasses on top of her head. "I can surprise you. I'm not a pampered princess."

"Could have fooled me."

"Look, I'm not used to this. The most freedom I've ever had in my life is this right now, away from my parents. There's always something expected of me, and I find it hard at times."

He ran a hand down his face and stared at her. "You going to talk about what was said yesterday?" Brass hated sounding like a pussy.

"I, er, I figured he was lying because he found me a nuisance. I don't really know what to do with my time. I'm used to being ordered around. Never thought I'd actually consider it a comfort to do as I'm told." She sighed.

Brass saw the sadness in her eyes, and it was like a kick to the gut.

"Would you like some breakfast?" he asked.

"Sure. I can eat. I love eating. It's what I do best."

Dumping his coffee in the nearest trashcan, he followed her into Mac's diner, and took a seat near the window.

"So, you're part of an MC. I've heard a lot about you guys since I've been in town. Good and bad stuff."

"You ever met an MC member before?"

"No." She picked up a menu. "My father only allowed us to associate with the *right* people as he called it. It was so embarrassing. My sisters and brothers were always happy to do the right thing, the stuff they accepted. Not me. It has been rather stifling."

"You're interesting."

"I'm a pampered princess who escaped her family by buying a shit car that has since broken down on me. Do you think it's fate?"

"Fate?"

"You know, like my destiny is that I'm to break down in this town, and I don't know, get a job, become independent so when I go home, I'll be able to walk on my own two feet."

Brass was starting to see this woman was talkative. Usually, he hated women that talked and talked. With Eliza, he wasn't getting the feel. He wanted her to talk, and he wanted to be the one to listen.

"I want to fuck you," he said.

There was no point in denying the person he was. She was never going to get flowers, roses, or any of that kind of shit from him. He was hardcore, and he wanted her pussy.

Eliza paused, and her cheeks flushed. "Are you always this blunt?"

"Yep. I fuck, and I like to fuck hard."

She laughed. "I'm kind of nervous."

"I'm not going to hurt you, and I'm also not going to force you. I've told you exactly what I wanted, so now it's up to you."

"You've told me you want to fuck me. What the hell do I have to do?" she asked.

"That's up to you. Fate brought you to Vale Valley. It made your car break down several feet from the shop where I was. You're here exploring your rebellion."

"I may be getting married."

"You don't even have a clue if you're getting married. Are you in a relationship?" he asked.

"No."

"Then I don't see a reason why we can't explore this thing between us, baby. Let me go and order." Brass made his way toward the counter, and when he checked the mirror, he saw she was still sitting at the table. *Interesting.* He hadn't made her run yet. It had to be a record for him.

Smiling to himself, he paid for several rounds of pancakes and coffee.

Settling back down opposite her, he saw her cheeks were flushed.

"I'm not a virgin."

"That's good. It means I don't have to take my time."

"Are you always going to be an ass?"

He shrugged. "If you want hearts and flowers, look elsewhere."

"I didn't come looking for you."

"No, but you've got me, and if you weren't interested, you'd have run away screaming."

She frowned. "Why does anyone like you?"

Brass chuckled. "Baby, I'm an asshole. I know what I want, and you know what, my heart is in the right place. My club brothers, they know I'll jump in front of a bullet for them. They don't need me to prove that I will. I'll just fucking do it. I will die for those I love and care about."

"For those you don't?"

"I've already got enough people to keep safe."

"Are you like the enforcer?"

"I'm not the enforcer. I'm just a brother who takes care of the club. We've all got our place."

Pancakes arrived, and Brass noticed there was no sign of Mary, which was strange.

"If I decide to do this, what are the rules?"

"No love, no relationship, just pure sex. We have it safe. I don't want any Brasses or Elizas running around our feet."

"I'm not ready for kids either. Don't worry, I wouldn't expect anything from you." She gave him a tight smile.

Even as they ate their pancakes, Brass wondered if she'd even consented to them fucking.

****

Mary entered the clubhouse, and the scent of cigarette smoke, vomit, and alcohol was overwhelming. She rushed toward a window and opened it up, hoping for some fresh air.

"Fucking kill me now," Duke said, lifting up from the long booth, and looking like death.

"Does Holly know where you are?" Mary asked.

"Of course she does. I sent her lots of texts." He lifted his phone up, and Mary leaned over reading them.

Duke: **I love you baby. I love you so much.**

Duke: **youre the best thing that happed to me.**

Mary smiled as she saw several of the texts started to look less romantic.

Duke: **bab weeee neeeeeed more kidzas**

"Flattering."

"Fuck me, my head is pounding, and it's all your fault."

Mary didn't dispute him. She had been in the wrong about so much stuff. It was entirely her fault, and she took the blame.

"Where is he?"

"In his room. He called it a night."

"Was he alone?" Mary asked.

Duke glared at her. "Yeah, he was alone. He had a chance to fucking walk out on you, and he didn't. You don't know how lucky you are to have a man like him."

"Enough, Duke," Pike said, startling the two of them.

She turned toward the doorway, seeing the man she had fallen in love with a long time ago.

"Pike," she said.

"I wouldn't ever step out on you, baby. I'm not going to lie, there was a part of me that wanted you to pay."

Tears filled her eyes. She deserved it.

"I love you too damn much to step out on you."

"I quit last night," she said.

"What?"

"I went to see Mac, and I, um, I found out the truth that you've been telling me. I was a fool. I didn't see it, and I didn't love him, nor did I want to ever do this between us. I love you. I completely, totally, love you. No one else will ever do for me." She released a breath. "I just wanted you to know. I gave him back the deeds to the diner. I'll work with Holly on my blog. Just expect a lot more experimenting from me," she said, laughing.

Pike rushed toward her, cupping her face. "You quit?"

"I quit. I loved working there, and Mac was just a friend. I love you, Pike. There was no interest on my part. The only man I've ever loved is standing right in front of me." She pressed her lips against his. "Love, love, love, love, love you," she said.

"You guys are making me sick," Landon said, popping up from the floor. "Mary, I swear, Pike is a fucking menace. You've got to keep him on a leash. I think I'm going to throw up."

"You made them all drink with you?" she asked.

"Of course. Let's go home, and keep me locked up safe before they all come to, and they're ready to kick my ass."

"I'm going to kick your ass. I'm going to send Holly to you. She'll do a better job of it than me."

****

Eliza stared down at her cell phone, which was ringing with her father's face flashing across the screen. She was getting ready for her first lunch shift at the diner, and she was looking forward to it. Working was something she enjoyed. Her siblings had always been happy for their parents to earn money. Her brothers were allowed to be part of the family business, but she and her sisters had to deal with finding a partner that was suitable for them. She hated the double standards.

Now they were trying to arrange her marriage for her. All of her life she'd never been like them. She'd never needed the finest things in life even though she'd been bought them. Eliza went through life feeling guilty. She didn't need the fine things. If she didn't wear them, her parents were upset, but wearing them made her feel like a hypocrite. She didn't need to wear them just because she could wear them.

People at school considered her an outcast as she wasn't desperate for the latest gadgets or even for the celebrity way of life. Most of the girls her own age were already thinking about how they could become famous. Sex tapes seemed to be the in thing, and she wasn't interested in those.

Taking the call, she pressed the cell phone to her ear.

"She answered, Eliza answered," her father said.

"Hey, Dad," she said.

"Baby, what is all this nonsense? Come home where you belong."

"You think I belong at home."

"Yes. We want you home, and Darcy can't wait to see you."

"Dad, I don't care about Darcy."

"Honey, there's no need to make any rash decisions right now. Come home, and we'll talk about this."

"We can organize the wedding another day," her mother said in the distance.

Her family weren't going to listen to her, none of them were. Letting out a breath, she closed her eyes and rubbed at her temple.

All of her life she had been controlled by what they wanted. "I just wanted to call you to let you know

I'm okay. I'm happy, and you don't need to worry about me."

"Seriously, Eliza, this has gone far—"

"Talk to you later." She hung up the phone and let out a breath. She'd never known how exhausting it was handling her parents. For the past week of being stranded in Vale Valley, she'd experienced a lot of fun. She'd been saving money out of her account for months, not to mention the money she'd earned waiting tables. In the beginning she'd been an awful waitress, and it had taken time for her to learn the ropes. Once she did, no one wanted her to leave.

Brass.

Her thoughts went back to the interesting biker who saw more inside her than she thought was possible.

A relationship with him, or a sex thing with him, would be so good. She wanted the chance to do that, to take her complete rebellion, and not look back with regret.

Leaving her small hotel room, she made her way toward the diner. It would be nice to walk on the wild side.

Chapter Ten

Knuckles entered the clubhouse with a smile on his face. He'd enjoyed a wonderful night, a perfect morning, and this evening, he was taking Beth out to a nightclub. It had been a long time since he'd been to a nightclub, and he hoped to make Beth enjoy it.

Daisy stood from the bar, and he looked pissed.

The club was opened up with windows letting in a breeze. Knuckles was covered in engine grease, and he stank from the day's work.

"I don't want any trouble," Duke said, coming in behind him.

"There won't be trouble when he stops seeing my sister," Daisy said.

He sighed. "I'm not doing her any harm."

"You're not? Beth doesn't know what she wants. She came to Vale Valley to escape the asshole who hurt her, and now you're saying to me that you know what she wants more than anyone else?"

"No, I'm saying that *Beth* knows what she wants, and she wants me!"

"You? You don't even have any respect for women. You work your way through them like they mean nothing."

"I could say the same about you, asshole," Knuckles said, stepping up toward Daisy. "You were fucking women even when Maria was here. Me, I haven't touched a single pussy but that of your sister."

Daisy's fist connected with his jaw. Knuckles saw it coming, and he let him have it. If Daisy needed a fight, then he'd give him one. He wasn't about to be pushed around, nor was he going to let Daisy think he was hurting Beth. He fucking loved her.

Getting up, he charged toward Daisy, lifting him up, and slamming him down on the nearest table.

"For fuck's sake, you two are just going to be complete assholes about this," Duke said.

Daisy kicked out at him, and Knuckles grabbed his feet, dragging him down. Suddenly, something hit his legs, and he went down. Daisy had grabbed a pool stick, and whacked him with it.

Holding a chair, he smashed it over Daisy, and they both rolled away, getting up.

"What do you want us to do?" Chip asked.

"They're fucking fighting inside, and the old ladies are going to be pissed," Landon said.

"Make them fucking move," Russ said. "We've not long changed furniture, and I don't want to take the girls shopping."

Knuckles slammed Daisy backward, and they hurtled them both into the kitchen. Grabbing the mixer, similar to the one he'd bought Beth, he threw it at Daisy, only for the brother to duck. He grabbed shit, and they started throwing things at each other.

"Get out of my wife's fucking kitchen," Duke said, hollering each word.

Knuckles was grabbed and dragged outside. Together they fought until with one blow from him, they both were flung back, separating. Getting to his feet, he glared at Daisy.

"I love her."

"You don't know the first thing about love."

"I don't? What about you? You're not known for being Mr. Fucking Love."

"I love Maria. She's my other half."

"Beth owns me, Daisy. She owns my soul, and I will fucking die for her. Do you understand? That's how much I fucking love her. I'll do anything for her."

Knuckles dropped his arms. "I won't fight you. Ask Beth. If she tells you that I'm pressuring her, then I'll back away, and I won't try to see her. Talk to Beth, not me."

Daisy stared, and even as they were panting, bleeding, and bruised, Knuckles saw him nod.

"Fine, I'll talk to my sister."

"You stupid fucking asshole," Duke said, coming outside. "Which one of you is going to call the women here, huh? Which one is going to explain that your fucking pissing contest has just ruined the fucking clubhouse?"

"You could have ended it," Knuckles said. Duke was a hard ass, and he'd easily defeat all of them. It was what made him a good Prez.

"You wanted me to get between the two of you, and what? Let this shit build up until it became something more?" Duke rubbed his eyes. "Tomorrow morning, Beth comes here, and so do the women. You two can answer to the shit that just went down. Knuckles, out that way, Daisy, out that way."

Treating them like children being ordered around, Duke took charge and sent them to opposite exits.

"I haven't gotten changed."

"Shower at your woman's place. Right now, I don't want to see either of you. Tomorrow morning, and this shit will finally get cleared up."

Knuckles got on his bike and headed toward Beth's apartment building. By the time he made it to her door, he was hurting, and the bruises were starting to come out. The smile on her lips disappeared when she caught sight of him. "What the hell?" she asked.

"Sorry, got into a little disagreement with your brother. He looks just as bad."

She helped him toward the shower, and together

they removed his clothes. "You look a mess." She ran her fingers down the back of his thighs. "What did this?"

"A pool stick, fucker grabbed it, and whacked the back of my legs."

"I can't believe he'd do something like this."

"I can." He turned the shower on and hissed as the cold spray hit him in the face. It was too much, and yet he didn't even try to move away. "He's only worried about you, for good reason as well."

"I'll tell him. I haven't seen him for a few days. I'll make sure I do."

"We have to go tomorrow morning."

"Why?" she asked.

"Because Daisy and I, we kind of fucked up the state of the clubhouse. As our punishment, we're being forced to go and face the wrath of the old ladies."

She nodded. "I don't have a washing machine. I'll go and put these down in the laundry room."

Knuckles realized she was dressed to go to a nightclub, and he hated the fact he'd spoiled it.

"We'll go another time to the nightclub."

"I can wait. It's fine." She smiled at him, and he watched her head out.

"Come back as soon as you can."

"Will do."

He stayed under the water, washing away the grime. Minutes passed, and he waited for Beth to return. When she did, he smiled. "There's plenty of room for you here, baby."

She stepped into the shower, and he tugged her against him. They weren't going to a nightclub, but he had her all to himself. The night was still young.

****

"Have you seen what you've done?" Holly asked. "You've destroyed nearly three thousand dollars' worth of equipment. Ugh!"

Beth was covered in an apron and gloves, and was going helping to clean up the mess of broken glass. Knuckles was in the main room with Daisy, listening to all of the women screaming.

"I didn't have anything to do with this," Pike said.

"I know, baby." Mary leaned over, kissing him deeply. "That's why you're not getting yelled at."

The couple had resolved their differences, and looked close together.

Moving through the main room, Beth caught sight of her brother, and instead of waiting for privacy, she stepped up to him. "You did this because of me?" she asked.

Knuckles stopped cleaning, and she was aware of all the nosy men paying them close attention. She didn't care. She wasn't about to stop her rant until her brother was aware of what she felt for Knuckles.

"Beth, you're not ready for a relationship."

"And who are you to decide, huh? You're my brother, not my keeper. I'm grateful for what you did getting Benedict to confess, but this is my life. I know what I want, and I want Knuckles."

She poked her finger against her brother's chest. "This is not your decision. This is mine."

"You see that! She wants Knuckles and you caused all this crap for nothing. Asshole!" Holly glared.

Duke was trying to look just as stern, but Beth didn't see it. If anything, he looked hungry.

Moving to Knuckles' side, she wrapped her arm around his waist. "This is my choice, it's not by force, or anything else. I want to be with him. Please, try to be happy, or at the very least, accept what I want from my own life. I want him."

Daisy sighed. "This is my fault. Maria, she tried to tell me, and I didn't listen." He looked at Knuckles, and then at her. "I'm sorry for behaving the way that I did. I'll leave you to make your own decisions and to accept them."

"Thank you. If you'd just come to me, you wouldn't be dealing with Holly, and she is pissed."

Beth moved past them, taking a large bag of trash out. When she turned to go back inside, she saw Daisy was there.

"I'm sorry," he said.

"I am, too."

"I see a difference in you. Knuckles is bringing that out of you, isn't he?"

"He is." She smiled. "Don't start any more fights because you think I'm hurting or something. I'm not. I'm really happy. I'm the happiest I've been in a long time, and I hope you can see it."

"I do."

He opened his arms, and she went into them willingly. "It's kind of hard to cope with you sleeping with one of my friends."

"Join the club. Maria's mine, and you still did her."

They both chuckled. "I guess we should tell our folks that we're still on good terms."

"Why? I haven't told them. I hope you didn't, unless you called them up to tell on me." She looked at Daisy and glared. "You didn't."

"I may have."

"Daisy! Now they're going to want us to visit."

"They're coming this Sunday. It's going to be the whole club. Mary and Holly have it all planned—"

"We *had* it all planned," Holly said, storming out. "Some asshole ruined all of our equipment. I don't know if I'll be ready in time, and I haven't got to go shopping."

Holly kept on ranting as she walked into the house. Following behind her, Beth paused near Knuckles, and pressed her lips against his as she passed.

"You okay?"

"I'm great. Never better." She gave him a quick hug, and then made her way toward the kitchen.

For the next few hours, they were cleaning up the mess. Mary and Holly ordered the equipment they needed online, and throughout it all, they moaned. When the brothers were about to complain about the price, they gave them both a look that had her laughing.

Pike set up the barbeque, and she went with Maria to go grab some food from the local supermarket. On the way inside the clubhouse, she saw Clinton driving in.

Grabbing the brown sacks, she looked toward him. "Is everything okay, boss?" she asked.

"I need to talk to Duke."

"He's around back, I think." Beth made her way toward the back of the clubhouse where most of the guys were sitting, shirts off, and drinking a beer. Knuckles moved up behind her and frowned at Clinton.

"You becoming a Trojan? You're going to have to wait in line. We've got a lot of guys wanting the job," he said.

Clinton shook his head. "I want to hire you."

"What?" Duke asked, stepping forward. He held Bell in his arms, and he didn't look too impressed to see her boss there.

"I've got a case. It's a really serious one." Clinton turned toward her. "I've been keeping it a secret, but she needs some help, and it's the kind of help I can't give her." He handed the file over to Duke.

Beth nibbled her lip as she watched Duke. He

opened the file and stared back up at Clinton. "Is this a fucking joke?"

"I wish it was. I can't offer her protection, but you can."

Duke closed his eyes, and Holly moved toward his side, taking Bell from him. "What's going on?"

"Clinton wants us to protect Maya Abelli. The little Italian mafia princess, current location unknown."

"She's in protective custody, but they can't take care of her."

"Church," Duke said. "Now."

Beth watched as Duke grabbed the back of Clinton's shirt, and started to drag him toward the clubhouse. She watched Knuckles, Daisy, Pike, Landon, all of the men as they made their way toward the clubhouse.

"What the hell just happened?" Beth asked.

"Something bad," Holly said, glancing toward her mother. "Have you ever heard of Abelli?"

Sheila went pale. "Many years ago, I did."

"Is this bad?"

"If Abelli never finds out, we're fine. If he does, we're all dead."

"Fuck!" Beth said, looking back at the clubhouse. *Double fucking fuck.*

****

Knuckles closed the door and turned in time to see Duke slam Clinton into the seat. "Of all the irritating fucking things I've seen in my life, this is really fucking priceless." He threw the file onto the table, pictures of Maya spilling out. Knuckles winced as her bruises, battered, broken body covered several of them. Pie picked them up and whistled.

"Someone clearly has issues. These are downright nasty. I haven't seen this kind of shit in a long time."

"Look, Maya saw a murder, okay? She saw several fucking murders. They killed her friends and her friends' kids. She couldn't take it anymore, so she took refuge with a cop. They did everything they could to try to keep her identity a secret. The fuckers used her as a plant, a source of information."

"Do I look like a give a fuck? MC and mafia don't fucking mix, you piece of shit. Is this for some fucking glory? To be the small town prick that did this?"

"This fell in my lap."

Knuckles had to give Clinton credit, he wasn't running away like a little bitch, screaming. He was facing Duke head on.

"It mysteriously fell in your lap?"

"I got a call from an old friend in the city. Said there was a woman, needed my help. Possible domestic dispute. I went to the hospital, and I was dragged in there, and then ordered to silence. Maya is in deep shit. The stuff she knows, she has the evidence that can put the Abelli family away for fucking life. You got me? Life. They're trying to keep her quiet."

"Do you want to know why the Abelli are still walking around?" Duke asked.

"They've got connections in high places."

"Everyone and everything that touches so-called informants, or rats, end up fucking dead!" Duke slammed his fist down on the table.

"She's innocent in this."

"Innocent? No one in the mafia is innocent. They breed monsters."

"Holy shit," Pie said, looking up.

"What? What is it?"

Knuckles saw that he'd gone pale. "What?"

"Did you see the age of her?" Pie asked.

Duke frowned, and Pie slid the file across.

Knuckles watched as Duke went pale.

"She's fifteen years old, and those pictures were taken a year ago."

Staring at the pictures, Knuckles took a long look, and he saw her immaturity.

"The Feds used a fucking girl!"

"It was some fucking rookie, okay?" Clinton said. "Why do you think I'm here? They're trying to clean up their mess, or at least one good cop is."

"Cop?"

"Yeah, my guy, he's a cop from the city, and he's the one that alerted me to all of this."

"You can't let her go to someone else," Russ said. "She's as good as dead."

"She comes here, we put our women at risk."

"The fact that Clinton is even here, we're at risk. The Abelli will come, and when they do, they'll kill everyone who ever heard of Maya. We're dead either way," Russ said, taking a seat. "I feel very old."

Knuckles stared at Duke, who had turned toward the window. Even from the door, he saw the women outside. The moment Clinton accepted that client and walked into their clubhouse with that folder, he'd changed all of their lives.

"No one ever comes back alive from the Abelli," Duke said. "I hate this."

"You walk away, it may not come back," Raoul said. "Get rid of Clinton, walk away."

Knuckles looked toward Raoul, and saw that he couldn't walk away.

"It's a kid," Crazy said. "What if it was Bell, or Matthew, or fucking Strawberry and Starlight? We can't walk away, not with a kid."

Knuckles thought about Beth. What kind of man would he be if he walked away, and allowed this girl to be hurt? He wouldn't be good enough for her.

"I'm in," he said, drawing the attention to him. "We can't let her go. She's a kid, and last time I checked, we were all fucking assholes, but not like that." He pointed toward the file. "I can't look at Beth if I let anything happen to that little girl."

"She was only trying to do what was right," Clinton said.

"You shut the fuck up." Duke looked at the room. "The vote has to be unanimous. If one of you votes no, then it's no."

"What do we do with her when she turns up? She can't have the same name," Landon said.

"Her name's going to be Winter."

"Sheila and I can't have a reason to call her ours," Russ said. "We're too old, and they know we wouldn't abandon her."

"Nor I," Duke said. "I killed my fucking wife, and I wouldn't leave a kid behind."

Knuckles watched as they all had a struggle as to how Maya was about to fit into their lives. If she was to be protected they had to have a reason for her to be with them.

"Then she can be my sister," Landon said, speaking up.

They all turned toward him.

"I'm not from around Vale Valley. I haven't given much of myself away. I show up with a girl, treat her like a sister, no one is going to know the difference. She can stay at the club. We can make it work."

"I don't understand," Clinton said. "You only need to protect her."

"'Only need to protect her' is easy if you haven't settled down, and have roots. We all have roots in Vale Valley. You tell me how we're supposed to blend in a

girl who just turns up one day. A sister will work. It has
to."

Chapter Eleven

One week later

Knuckles sat at the clubhouse with Beth by his side. It had been a week since Clinton's visit. He rubbed at his temples as he cleared the sleep from his eyes. It was a Friday night, and they'd just returned from their drug run. He was tired, and wary. All of the brothers were. There was not the usual bravado, nor the same lightness within the club.

He imagined once Maya—or Winter, as they had to call her—came, they'd be tense for a long time.

"What's wrong?" Beth asked.

Duke had ordered them to keep the information to themselves until he was ready for others to know. First, Duke wanted to establish Winter in the fold, and to make sure everything was safe and secure.

Knuckles had even gone with Duke to buy some weapons. They all owned their own, and kept a small supply in the basement, but with Winter came a threat, so it was time to start getting serious.

"Nothing, babe, I'm just tired."

He tugged her down into his lap, kissing her neck.

"You can tell me anything," she said.

"I know." As a way to let off steam, Knuckles had taken her to his old club where he'd trained with the best Doms around. Beth had been a little uncomfortable at first in the club. Knuckles hadn't made a move for more to happen. He wanted her to watch, and to also see how she responded to certain scenes.

"Everyone is tense," she said.

"It's okay." He breathed in her scent, trying to fill every single sense with her. She was his entire world.

"So, when are you guys going to make honest people out of yourselves?" Raoul asked, sitting with Zoe at his side.

"Huh?" Beth said.

"In the eyes of the club, you going to take her as your old lady or what?" Raoul put his arm around Zoe's shoulders, and Knuckles wanted to hurt him. With everything going on around the club, the last thing he needed to deal with was Raoul.

"Seriously, you're talking about that with my sister."

"She knows about it. I've seen her watching that when she lived here."

"Please kill me now." Beth buried her face against his chest.

"What the heck are you doing?" Pie asked.

"Everything is supposed to be normal right?" Raoul asked, giving them all pointed looks. "I'd say right now we're looking at little out of place for our regular Friday night."

"Speaking of, where is Landon?" Zoe said. "He told me there was someone he wanted me to meet. I'm going to be totally surprised, and blown away."

"I've got to get a beer," Knuckles said. He got to his feet, and made his way into the clubhouse. Raoul followed him in. "This isn't a laughing matter."

"Dude, I already spoke to Duke and the others. We all look ready to fucking pounce. This is supposed to be a house of protection. This is about us looking fucking normal. Do it, otherwise we're going to look suspicious."

"You expect me to take Beth as my old lady with this shit?"

"That's precisely my point, Knuckles. What shit? To everyone else, Landon's sister is here to visit, and nothing is out of fucking order. You're acting like we're about to die, and maybe we are. We're not supposed to know."

Knuckles saw his point, so he nodded. "Fuck."

"Yeah, fuck. I know it's hard, and it's tense, but we got to try, you know?"

Taking two beers out, Knuckles paused as he saw Landon had his arm thrown across a woman's shoulders. She had dark brown hair, so dark it looked almost black, and she looked slender.

Showtime. Moving toward his woman's side, Knuckles handed her a beer and tugged her close.

"Knuckles, this here is my sister. I tried to keep her away, but Winter didn't want to be left alone anymore."

"Nice to meet you, Winter," he said.

"You as well."

She didn't have an accent, and she smiled at him. He saw she looked nervous.

"I can't believe Landon never talked about you," Zoe said. "Didn't you say you were an only child?"

"He wishes he was. Clearly, he's not. He doesn't like it that I'm way smarter than he is," Winter said.

"She seems nice," Beth said.

"I know."

"I read her file," Beth said quietly, startling him.

"What?"

"This is what has you stressed out?" Beth asked.

"Beth, babe, I don't—"

She stood up and held her hand out, which he took. He followed close behind her as she took him upstairs toward his room. Knuckles closed the door, and turned toward Beth.

"You don't what?" she asked.

"We shouldn't be talking about it."

"Orders from Duke to keep it silent?"

"It's dangerous."

"I'm not mad at you," she said. "I read the file, and I knew why you couldn't tell me. Abelli."

"You didn't research the name, did you?"

"No. I didn't. I didn't have to. They're in the newspaper. How did she stay out of it?" Beth asked.

"They kept her hidden. The Abelli know how to keep their secrets. I wanted to tell you."

"You couldn't. I can keep a secret, Knuckles, and I don't blame you."

He cupped her face, staring into her blue eyes, and he sighed. "I'm in love with you," he said.

"What?"

"You're a witch, there's no doubt about it. You've gotten under my skin, and into my heart. I don't know how you did it. I don't want to live without you."

She giggled. "That's good, because I love you, too, and I don't want to live without you."

He slammed his lips down on hers, and she melted against him.

"How about we go back home?" he asked.

"Or we can stay right here," she said, moving toward his closet.

Knuckles watched as she pulled out one of his boxes. She opened it up and retrieved a pair of cuffs.

"It's not much, but it's a start. What do you think?"

"You want me to cuff you?"

"You can do whatever you want with me," she said.

She was so much temptation wrapped in a beautiful blonde package. "Get naked."

Beth removed her clothes, and Knuckles watched.

What he didn't expect was for her to sink to her knees before him, submitting to him.

Moving forward, he stroked his fingers through her silky strands. "You're so beautiful, and pretty. Look at me." She tilted her head back, and he smiled. "Get up."

She got to her feet, and he spun her around, securing her hands behind her back. "Do you trust me?" he asked.

"Completely."

"Good." He pushed her down to the bed, and ran his hands down her back. "Are you ready to be my old lady?" he asked.

"Yes."

"Are you sure? I don't want you thinking this has a get out clause. It doesn't. Once you're mine, and declare us to the club, that's it. No second chances."

"I want to belong to you, Knuckles, so much."

"Good, because there's no doubt about it, baby, you're mine." He ran his hand down her back, and she wriggled, trying to get closer to his hand. Smiling, he slapped her ass, then slipped his hand between her thighs to find her soaking wet already.

"Please," she said.

"I love it when you beg." He thrust his fingers inside her cunt and started to pump in and out.

"So good," she said.

Releasing her hands, he put her into position on her knees, and made her stay there so that he could see.

Releasing his cock, he tore into a condom, and slid it over his length.

Moving behind her, he gripped her bound hands and lifted her up. Finding her entrance, he slammed home. They both cried out together.

"Who's in control of you, baby?" he asked.

"You are, always you."

"Good. No matter what, I'll always take care of

you."

"I know."

He loved her even more for her complete faith in him. Knuckles would go to the ends of the earth to keep her safe. No matter what threat came from Winter, he'd protect the club, and his woman.

Pulling out of her tight heat, he slammed back home, fucking her with a force that startled them both.

All the fears leaked out of him, and he claimed what was his, the woman that belonged to him.

"I love you, Beth, so damn much."

It was quick, fiery, and shocking as they came together. Knuckles kissed her neck, putting his mark on her for everyone to see.

****

Life remained normal for the Trojans in Vale Valley. Beth didn't see anything go awry, and she never let on that she knew about Winter's true identity. Clinton continued to work, and Winter actually enrolled in the school. Daisy and Knuckles stopped fighting, and her parents even accepted Knuckles into the fold, which was a welcome relief. She couldn't have handled her parents not liking him.

Maria and Daisy were also expecting a new baby, and Matthew was home for the fall vacation. It was getting cold, and because of how crazy life had gotten, Knuckles hadn't initiated the old lady claiming, which seemed totally wrong to her, but who was she to judge?

It was a Friday, and she'd finished work early, and was heading out of the office when Knuckles startled her from behind.

"Hello, beautiful."

"What are you doing?"

"Well, I was surprising you."

"This is kind of scary. It's not a nice surprise at

all."

"Why not?" he asked.

"You scared me a little."

He leaned forward, nibbling her neck. "Sorry, baby, I didn't mean to startle you." He released her eyes, and he smiled. "What's wrong?"

"Nothing."

"Beth, I know you, and something is wrong. What is it?"

"Do you want me to be your old lady?" she asked, feeling stupid.

"Yeah."

"Okay." She walked past him, and he grabbed her arm, pulling her back.

"No, it's not okay, and you're going to spoil my surprise. With the club, life has been pretty hectic, and I haven't been able to do everything that I've wanted to do. Also, Daisy hasn't exactly made life easy either, and I'm not going to fight your brother."

"I don't want you to."

"However, I've told the guys that tonight is the night. I'm claiming you, and I don't give a fuck what Daisy thinks."

"I'm going to be your old lady?"

"To me, you already are, but the club has this tradition. I think it's crazy, but it makes sense."

She squealed, wrapping her arms around him. "I never thought I'd be this excited for exhibitionism."

"Haha, they'll only see what I want them to see."

"I love you, Knuckles."

"Baby, you don't have the first clue how I feel about you, but that's okay, I can show you in time."

She did know, and now that she was going to be his old lady, she was more than happy to wait till tonight. She was nervous—who wouldn't be?—but she was also looking forward to it. Finally, she was going to belong to him.

"What changed your mind?" she asked.

They walked hand in hand toward his bike. Beth had been for many rides on his bike, and it had to be one of the most amazing experiences of her life.

"With everything going on, I didn't want to have you commit to me if something went wrong."

"Like what?"

"Like me dying. I want you to be able to go, to leave, and not have to worry."

She paused at his bike and turned to cup his face. "Knuckles, I'd never run from you or away from you. I'm in this for life."

"It's dangerous."

"So? I lived my life trying to be safe once, and that didn't work. I want to be wherever you are."

Knuckles stroked her cheek, and she held onto his hand, smiling. "I'm never letting you get away."

"Besides, you've still got a challenge right now."

"Oh yeah, and what's that?"

"You've still got to go all Dom on my ass. I'm hoping it will be real soon. I want to see what all the fuss is about. My own brother warned me against you. It made me wonder if you hadn't taken a whip to him."

"Ha, you'd think it." He handed her the helmet, and she stuck her tongue out. Once it was on, Knuckles smiled at her. "How do you know I haven't been going all Dom on your precious ass?"

"I'd know."

"I once told you there was more to being a Dom than whips, leather, and chains. You shouldn't believe everything you read." He climbed on his bike, leaving her with a lot more questions than she had answers.

Straddling the bike, she wrapped her arms around

him and held on tightly. Where had he been going all Dom on her? Besides the time in the bedroom where she'd handed him the cuffs, there hadn't been much else.

The ride to her apartment was short, and she wished she didn't have to wear the damn helmet. She always found it way too constricting.

Climbing off, she removed the helmet, and he took it from her, holding her hand as they made their way upstairs toward her apartment.

"Okay, I want to know what you mean about being Dom on me. I've been thinking about it, and I can't *not* think about it."

He chuckled. "I figured that would give something to distract you all the way home."

They entered her apartment, and she went straight to the bedroom. Knuckles stood in the doorway with his arms folded.

"I don't get it."

"Look, Daisy knows that side of me. It's all he's ever known. Once the brothers heard that I trained as a Dom, and that I enjoyed it, that was it for them. I was a Dom, and nothing else."

"I don't understand."

"A Dom is a Dominant man, meaning he likes control. I take control, and you embrace that control."

"I still don't understand."

"I've been guiding you. I helped with you getting that job with Clinton, and I checked to make sure he was safe. Fucking asshole should stay away from prank or mystery callers, but there we go. In the bedroom I take control. It's not all about whips."

"Do you like being a Dominant?" she asked, taking a seat on her bed.

"It's what I know, and it's what I can do." He sat down beside her, taking her hand. "I told you how

129

everything got started up. I'm not in desperate need to hit you with a whip." He chuckled, which started her off. "In the club, what you're known for, it gets heightened up. Yes, I'm a trained Dom, and I can hit your ass with a coiled whip so that it stung, and you wouldn't be able to sit down for a few hours. I've trained with the equipment by expert men and women. I'm not begging to tie you up, Beth. I'm not going to start looking for a woman who is a sub."

"You're not."

"It's an element that I like within the bedroom, but again, it's not what defines me. If someone was to ask who I was, I'd say I was Knuckles, a club brother, and your old man." He locked their fingers together, kissing her hand.

"Why didn't you ever dispute Daisy or the others?"

"What would be the point? They're only being fuckers. It's what they're known for, and it is kind of fun. Scrap that, it is fucking funny." He got to his feet. "There's a party tonight. I've bought you something." He moved toward their wardrobe. Knuckles had moved in with her, and she loved it.

At night with his arms wrapped around her, to Beth, was total enjoyment.

He pulled out a black skirt that would go to her knee, and a white sweater. Even though it looked conservative, it had a sexy appeal to it. "It's going to be cold out, and I don't want you sick after this."

"I've heard that this is like a marriage. Is that true?"

"You got it, babe. After tonight, we'll be married in the eyes of the club." He put the clothes on the bed and moved to stand in front of her. He tilted her head back and slammed his lips down on hers.

When he pulled away, she was already gasping for more.

"I thought I should warn you that the couples in our club were married soon after, so if I was you, I'd be expecting a proposal soon."

She jerked back. "What?"

"You heard," he said, smiling.

"You can't just spring that on a woman and walk away."

He got to the doorway and looked back. "I just did."

"When?" she asked, calling after him.

"When I'm ready to give you a ring."

Her heart was pounding. Knuckles was going to propose to her. When? She was excited.

She'd say yes. Of course she'd say yes. There was no reason not to.

Chapter Twelve

Holly walked into Duke's office at their home. She'd just put Bell and Drake down to sleep. It had been a few weeks since Winter had entered their lives, and she knew exactly what was going on. Duke didn't keep anything from her, and since Clinton had handed this to the Trojans, her husband had been spending a lot of time alone, thinking.

"You okay?" she asked.

"No."

Entering his office, she walked up toward him and placed her hand on his shoulders. "You shouldn't stress yourself."

"I shouldn't? I don't even believe for a second that Clinton even realizes what he's done. It's like a game to him."

"He's been here though, talking with you, and checking on Winter. He hasn't just dumped it into your lap."

"If they find out about her, there's going to be a lot of bloodshed."

She rubbed his shoulders. All of her life she had lived with that threat, and she was still here to tell the tale, and told him so.

"This is different."

"I don't know what to say to you to make it better." She pressed a kiss to his cheek. "Winter is still their daughter."

"And yet they set some men to rape and beat her, Holly. The mafia, they're not a bunch of kids looking for a fight."

She sighed and moved to sit no his knee. "Duke, look at me."

He turned his gaze toward her. "I don't know if I can protect you."

"You can protect me. We'll figure something out. We always do." She pressed her lips against his. "Remember, you're part of the Trojans, and you've got a long history for being deadly. Just because you've got a wife and kids, don't let that influence your life now. I can hold my own, and I'll stand by your side. Every single man in that club, they voted to protect this woman. I'd say you've got nothing to worry about, and remember, the mafia are just a bunch of men, like you."

He chuckled. "You're right."

"Of course I'm right. I'm your wife. Besides, how do you know the Abelli won't see this as some kind of, um, business arrangement? When Winter's old enough, she could marry one of the Trojans, and there you go, you're allies, not enemies. Isn't that the Trojan way?"

Duke gripped her hips and pulled her to straddle his waist, and she sank her fingers into his hair. "I love you, Holly."

"I know. I'm hot stuff." She took possession of his lips, rubbing her nose against his.

"You're not afraid?" he asked.

She released a sigh. "I'm a little afraid, not a lot. You once told me that it took a lot to scare you. I've got a feeling the Abelli don't scare you. Your family, they scare you."

"I've got a gun, and I can shoot any man, but I've got so many lives to protect."

"Now you see why my parents struggled so much. It was a huge decision for them both to make."

"Speaking of decisions, I've got to head to the club. Knuckles is finally making Beth his old lady, and I've got to be there."

She wrinkled her nose, recalling Darla's

initiation. "Old-lady-claiming is much nicer than club whores."

"There's a point to the club whores. They need to know they're part of one club, wanted by many men, but not one."

"It's coldhearted, don't you think?"

"It's cold, but the life they lead, it has to be a cold one. No brother wants a woman who spreads her legs for multiple men."

Holly shrugged. "Some men do. I don't judge."

Duke got to his feet. "Love you, Holly."

"Love you, too. Now, go be a perv, and watch a claiming."

Holly smiled as she watched her husband climb on his bike and head toward the clubhouse. Running fingers through her hair, she made her way back into her bedroom, where she had found the box that she'd possessed since she was a kid. Inside, there was a picture of a man, a man smoking a cigar, holding a glass of wine with an arm wrapped around her mother's shoulders. Holly stood, four years old, in front of them. Flipping the card over, she saw the writing: *Abelli, Sheila, and Holly.*

Ever since the Abelli name had been mentioned, it had been driving her crazy. She recognized the name, and memories, or images had invaded her.

Sitting back, she rested her head, and wondered what her mother would have to say about this.

****

"Do you want me to contact him?" Sheila asked.

Russ shook his head, staring down at the pictures of another lifetime, a lifetime that came long before he'd taken the reins of the Trojans. He'd been a Prospect who liked to mingle with the mafia. Russ had earned himself a place as a fighter, and into the mafia's good graces. They had even wanted him to become a soldier for them. He'd declined. Of course, he'd then met Sheila, and everything changed.

"Holly could remember. She'll have questions, and when he finds out that Maya is here…"

"Winter. Her name is Winter, and you're not going to contact him." Russ rubbed at his face, wishing he'd put the Abelli bastard in the ground when he had the chance. They always said that skeletons in the closet had a way of coming out, and his had just fucking arrived.

Was it coincidence?

Fuck, he'd tried to bury the past a long time ago.

"Look, Russ, you knew this was going to happen. The Abelli, they're going to come back, and when they do, our history is going to come to light."

"Our history, you mean the fact that I fell in love with you, even though you were with him? You were married to Abelli, had a fucking kid with him: Holly."

He gritted his teeth. Russ had a lot of regrets, but falling in love with Sheila wasn't one of them. He'd been a kid, and Abelli had started to fuck other women. Sheila had been kind, and to a point innocent. She hadn't completely understood what being married to Abelli meant, until she saw the kind of death and destruction her husband meted out. Russ didn't care what anyone said. Holly was *his* kid. He'd been there when she was first born, and he'd nurtured her right under her own father's nose.

Rubbing at his eyes, he shook his head.

Russ had gone at the Abelli all guns blazing, leaving only one man with the promise that if he ever came after them, he'd put a bullet in his head. The Abelli was on the other side of the world, and he had believed that he'd sent them to Italy.

There had been rumors, but over time, he'd started to feel safe.

"Winter is Holly's half-sister."

"I've got to tell Duke."

No one in the Trojans knew the truth. Russ had kept it secret, killing anyone who doubted.

Looking back, Russ had been an animal, a monster.

"Why did you fight so hard for me?" Sheila asked.

He looked toward the woman he loved. "What?"

She forced a smile. "You once said that I deserved to be happy, and yet, you cheated on me just like he did. Forget it."

"Do you regret our life together?" he asked, getting to his feet, reaching for her.

"I regret lying, Russ. This is what we've done. We have created a life together based on a lie. Holly, she's going to find out, and she's going to hurt because of it. Our past shouldn't cause these problems." Sheila sighed, turning away from him.

Grabbing the details he needed, Russ headed out to the clubhouse. His past was coming back to haunt him. He had walked away the victor, and now he didn't imagine he was going to get very far.

****

"You can put all of your girly shit there, and if you want we can go and get some pink paint. Girls like pink frilly shit," Landon said, looking around the room. Winter was staying at the clubhouse, and she stood in the doorway of her new room. "What do you think?"

"You stress out a lot."

"Yeah, never had a sister to take care of, and as strange as it sounds, I want to do this job properly."

She moved to sit on the bed. "It's nice, and it's loud."

"Loud?"

"Most of the time at home, we weren't allowed around many of my father's associates. My mother, she was always out of it on drugs and alcohol. I was alone a lot of the time. My dad screwed the nannies so they were always disappearing. It sucked."

"You lived a totally sucky life?"

"It wasn't always bad. I got to wear nice things, and most people at school were afraid of me. I had guards all the time. It was really weird. My dad would always say he lost a kid before. I figure it's because he's so violent during a woman's pregnancy," she said, shrugging.

"You do know for a fifteen-year-old girl to be talking about violence like that, it's not normal."

"I'm not normal. I'm the daughter of Abelli. Some of us are lucky to be born into a nice loving home, and others into violence." She shrugged. "We're handed problems left and right."

Landon took a seat on the bed, staring at the girl. She was fifteen years old, and yet she carried an intelligent conversation, which was new.

"You're doing that weird staring thing. Are you a creepo?"

"No. Girls don't do it for me. I'm more than happy to stick with a woman. Do you regret going to the cops?"

"I regret going to the wrong people. I don't know if you know this, but getting beat up isn't what the movies make out to be."

"We'll keep you safe here."

"No offense, Landon, I'm not safe anywhere. If my father wants to find me, he'll find me. He'll kill me when I no longer serve a purpose to him."

"Kill you? I thought you were already on the endangered list."

She laughed. "No. That, the beating and stuff, that was just me getting punished for being naughty. I'm a woman. I'm good to be sold into marriage." She snorted. "Over the years women are considered these waste-of-space items that men put up with. For parents, however, we're the ones that are used to make empires, through marriage. We're the most powerful beings on earth, we just don't know it."

"I'm thoroughly depressed."

"Sorry, when you spend time on your own, you tend to do a lot of thinking, reading, and watching. I loved documentaries, history, stuff like that."

"No romance there?"

"I've never believed in romance. I was never going to find someone to love, and I'm not going to start now. Sucks, doesn't it?"

"I'm not a romantic, and I find it sad you've only known violence."

"When my father comes for me, don't do anything stupid, okay?"

"Like what?"

"Like band together with him. My father's deadly unless there's something he wants, and then he'll do whatever he can to get it. From what I saw, Trojans possess nothing that would interest him."

"Hey, we're an interesting bunch of men."

She chuckled. "Okay, then."

"I'm heading downstairs. I'll be just across the hall." He moved toward the drawers beside her bed. "Here's a gun, and I read your file. You know how to use it. Anything happens, run, and use it."

"I will."

He left the bedroom and made his way downstairs. Brass was sitting at the table, nursing a beer.

"You okay?" Brass asked.

"Yeah, I'm fine. Women, they're fucking freaky." Landon waited for a beer to be put in front of him, and he took it, thankful for the distraction of the young girl upstairs. Landon felt protective of the girl. No one else had stood up for her during the whole of her life, and he wanted to be the man that was different from all of the others.

****

Knuckles held Beth's hand as they made their way around the outside of the clubhouse. Many of the club whores were out in full force, teasing the brothers. He spotted Leanna and Crazy dancing together.

"What's going to happen?" she asked.

"Just let it happen. It's what we all do. Let the music take you, and have some fun. It's no rush to get it over with." He wrapped his arm around her, dancing. It was cold out, and he offered her more of his warmth as they moved around several of the brothers.

"Are you ready to be an old lady?" Mary asked, coming up toward them.

"I am."

Pike moved up behind Mary, shaking his hand. Knuckles nodded at him. The brother had been in a better mood since Mary had finally come to her senses, and he was pleased. Knuckles didn't like to see any unrest at the club.

"Daisy stayed home," Pike said.

"That's good. Do you want a beer, babe?" he asked.

Beth shook her head. "Juice for me, or soda."

"Will do."

Walking with Pike, he made his way inside, passing Duke's office. Glancing inside, he saw a pissed off Duke and a worried Russ.

Pike sighed. "Don't you like club life better when

no one seems to give a fuck about what trouble is going down where?" he asked.

"I'd gladly take that shit." Knuckles went straight to the fridge, grabbing out a cool beer and an orange soda. "I want to propose to Beth, only I want to do it properly. What do you think?"

"Man, there's a whole lot of ways to propose to a woman. Beth's a simple kind of girl. Nothing elaborate."

"I've already asked Daisy, and her father."

"Fuck me, are you trying to be son-in-law of the year?"

"I want everything to be right."

"Did they at least give you your blessing?"

"Yes." Sipping his drink, he pulled the ring out of his pocket. "What do you think?" It was a simple diamond ring. The expense of it had been irrelevant.

Pike whistled. "Coming from you, I believe she's going to love it."

Knuckles sighed. "Were you nervous marrying Mary?"

"I'm nervous every single day I'm with Mary. We have our troubles, but like we've just proven, we come back fighting each time. She's the love of my life, and I wouldn't be with anyone else."

"I'm happy for you."

"Good."

They headed out toward their women who were now talking with Zoe, Darla, and Emma. Wrapping his arms around Beth, he kissed her neck, handing her a drink. For the next couple of hours, he got her to relax by talking with the guys, and the women. They danced, and when it was time, he took her into the clubhouse. The doors were locked behind them. Her protection meant everything. For all of the old ladies, the doors were guarded, and only a select few men were present.

Taking Beth into the clubroom, he kept on dancing with her. All the time the ring in his pocket continued to burn a hole. He wanted to propose, and he'd thought of putting it in her drink, even presenting it in her food. All had been overdone and a little tacky for him. There had to be a way to make her his, and it be perfect.

Tilting her head back, he stared into her eyes, sensing her discomfort and her embarrassment.

"This is a lot harder than I imagined," she said.

Knuckles sank to his knee before her. "I never in my whole life thought I'd find someone who meant as much to me as you do. I'm totally in love with you, and if you can't handle tonight, and you don't want to, I understand." He pulled the ring out of his pocket. "You'll be my old lady in my heart, and in life." Knuckles presented her the ring. "Marry me, Beth."

She gasped. "You said you weren't going to propose?"

"I said I would when I thought the moment was right. This is the right moment, now, in front of my club brothers, as you're about to become my old lady. If you don't want to do that, it's fine."

She sank to her knees, cupped his face, and took possession of his lips. "Even though it makes me uncomfortable, I'm going to do it. I'm going to do it for you, and because all of the other old ladies have done it. If I can't, what kind of old lady are you getting?" she asked.

Sliding the ring on her finger, he got to his feet, and took her toward the pool table. Many of the brothers had done this. Lifting her up, he eased her down and lifted up her skirt, touching the fabric over her pussy. She was wet, and he slipped his fingers inside to find her heat.

They both moaned.

"No one else will see you."

"I trust you, Knuckles. I love you, and I'll do whatever it takes to be by your side for the rest of our lives."

With the brothers around them watching, Knuckles removed a condom from his jeans and tore into the foil packet. He slid the latex over his length, preparing himself. Sliding his fingers down her slit, he got her nice and wet, and ready for his dick.

She moaned, wrapped her arms around his neck, and he found her cunt, sliding inside. With the brothers watching, Knuckles made love to her, holding her close as he let them know with his actions that no other man was allowed to touch her. Beth belonged to him, and as such, they had to give her the same treatment as the other ladies.

He surrounded her, never letting her know that a dozen sets of eyes were watching them.

"I love you, Beth," he said, finding his release before she found hers. Like many of the brothers before him, he picked his woman up and carried her upstairs to his room.

"You didn't have to carry me."

"Beth, you were amazing down there."

"I'm your old lady, and you can't get rid of me now."

"I don't intend to."

"We're going to get married," she said, with a squeal.

"Yep, we're going to get married, and one day soon we're going to have lots of babies, and life is going to be totally perfect."

"Are you sure?"

"Yes."

"I love you, Knuckles."
"Babe, I love you so damn much."

Chapter Thirteen

For the next few weeks, Beth organized their wedding, and made sure that Knuckles had no choice but to attend the cake testing and assist with the flower arrangements. They were going to use the church in town, and he was going to wear a tuxedo. She got him to extend invitations to the women who helped raise him.

"You know, all of this organizing, and it's making me wonder if you even love me, or love the thought of being married to me," Knuckles said, late one night.

She slapped his arm, and he tackled her to the floor, resulting in them getting nothing done but having a lot of sex, and carpet burns.

Maria was going to be her maid of honor, along with the old ladies being her bridesmaids. They were like a family, bound together by their men. Knuckles picked Daisy as his best man as he thought it was only worth it.

The tension within the club was still mounting. Duke and Russ argued daily, and there seemed to be something going on with Holly, but Beth didn't know what.

Two months passed, and Beth was growing disheartened with all of the organization that was involved in the wedding. He'd seen it happening to her, and so he wasn't surprised when late one Sunday night, she picked up all of her notebooks, and magazines, booklets, leaflets, everything, and launched it across the room.

Knuckles was entering their apartment as she did it.

It nearly hit him, and he quickly dodged it.

"Is there a reason you're throwing your stuff at

me?" he asked.

"I wasn't throwing it at you. I didn't want this, okay? I didn't want a wedding that made me sick to my stomach to look at cake, or another dress." She ran fingers through her hair, frustrated that she'd forgotten to brush it after her shower. In the manic that had become her life, she'd shaved one leg, and one armpit. Forgot to wash the soap off, and now her hair was all matted at the back. "I was not the kind of girl growing up who was desperate for a lavish wedding."

"What did you want then?" Knuckles asked, removing his jacket, and coming to sit with her. She moved, straddling his lap, as he grabbed her ass, cupping the cheeks. Their sex life was the best, and Knuckles had been exploring his more Dominant side within the bedroom, driving her crazy. She didn't realize that she had a submissive side, but he drew it out of her.

"It was pretty simple, church, dress, tuxedo, cake, party, honeymoon, lots of sex, marriage, ta-da, kids."

He laughed. "Simple?"

"Yeah, simple. I don't care if a red rose is going to ruin the display of white roses. Let's face it, Knuckles, you've taken my mouth, pussy, and ass. I'm way past being a virgin."

He snorted, which only made her glare at him.

"I don't want all of the crap of bridal fitting, bridal showers. Gifts are a must, but again, I don't care what we have. I just want to be your wife in the eyes of the law. Nothing more."

Knuckles sighed. "Trying to make an honest woman out of you, and you're complaining?"

"Do you want the big wedding? If you do, I'll go through it, and I'll punish us both for it. I promise."

"Babe, I want what you want. If you want the wedding, the live band and all of that shit, then have it.

This is going to be the only time you get married, so make sure it's exactly as you want it. Once we have what we want, there's no going back."

She smiled. "I want things simple, and to say 'I do' to you in front of our friends, and family."

"Then in the morning, that's exactly what we'll do. Simple, easy, fresh, and perfect." He took possession of her lips and ran his fingers inside her large sweatpants, finding her hot, wet core. Sliding his fingers inside her, he got them nice and wet, drawing them back to her ass. "You reminded me that I haven't taken your ass in a long time, and I think it's time you gave it to me."

"Knuckles?"

"No complaints, baby, we're having a simple wedding, and your husband needs attention." He removed his fingers and gave her instruction. "Go, get naked, and kneel on the bed with that ass up in the air. I want to see what belongs to me, and what has my name all over it."

He gave her a few minutes' head-start before following her in.

She was down on the bed with her ass up in the air. He went straight for the drawers nearest their bed, and took out the lube and a condom. They were keeping the condom companies up and running. They went through so many every single week.

Removing his clothing, he climbed on the bed behind her and opened up the lube.

"You love it when I take your ass, don't you, baby?" he said, getting his fingers nice and slick, ready for her ass.

"Yes."

The first time they'd done this, she tried to deny it. Her soaking wet cunt had shown them both she was lying, so he'd made her wait for her orgasm all day until he was ready for her punishment to be over.

Smearing the lube over her anus, he slid a finger inside, and using the tube, he pumped some more lube inside her.

She moaned, pushing back against him as she did. He rubbed more of the lube over his dick, and placed the tip against her ass, pressing forward. She tensed up at first, but doing as he always instructed, she pushed out, allowing him past that tight ring of muscles inside her.

"It's okay, baby, I've got you. It's okay."

"Oh, God."

"Not God, remember, Knuckles." He pressed every inch inside her, and she moaned.

He gripped her hips, running his hands up and down her curves, loving her.

Knuckles hadn't been picky. He'd have gone with the elaborate wedding, or something quiet, simple, and beautiful.

Providing he was with her, he didn't care about anything else.

They were bound together for the rest of their lives.

****

"You're leaving, then?" Brass asked, entering Eliza's hotel room.

She stopped her packing, and turned toward him. "I didn't hear you knock."

"I'm still at the door, which you left open. Not a smart move."

Eliza sighed. "My car was finally fixed. My piece of shit car sounds much better than the expensive one back at home."

"You didn't answer my question."

She sat down on the bed, and stared up at him. They'd been together for the past couple of months.

Yeah, her longest ever relationship in her life was with a biker she didn't intend to have a future with. What hurt the most was the past couple of months had been the best of her life. She didn't want to leave, but if she didn't, she was going to be broken when he moved on. Eliza was under no illusions. Brass *would* move on. She was surprised he'd even been interested in her. Not many people were.

"I don't know what you want me to say."

"You done? You going to run off."

"I'm not running anywhere."

"Did your Daddy call you? Want you to go and marry the guy he's picked out for you."

"Why are you being an asshole?" Her father called her all the time, and it sucked. He wasn't happy that she'd gone through this rebellion, and he wanted her back. Nothing she did was ever good enough, and to top things off, she had fallen in love with a man who only saw her as a quick fuck.

"That's who I am."

"Do you want me to stay? Is that what you're having trouble with dealing? I'm not sticking around. If you want me to stay, then tell me. Say, 'Eliza, stay.' I'm pretty good at following orders."

"Stay," he said, surprising her.

"What?"

"I'm not a brilliant man, okay? I'm not rich. I don't have a ton of wealth waiting for you. I'm not even sure I know how to fucking love, but I know I don't want you to go."

"Is this about the sex?"

"I can have sex anywhere, and with anyone, Eliza. Stay."

"With no promises?"

"We're having fun. Stay, have some fun with me,

and let's see where it goes."

Staring at her packed bag, she let out a sigh.

"What if I fall for you?" she asked, not daring to tell him the truth that she already had fallen for him.

"I'll be a complete and total asshole to you."

She smiled. Eliza liked him, asshole or not, she did. She was a fucking loser, loving a man who was an asshole.

"Then I'll stay. One day I'll have to go."

"That day isn't today." He walked into the hotel room and closed the door behind him. The way he flicked the lock had everything in her tensing. Her pussy grew slick, and all doubt ceased as he turned toward her. "You're going to be my date at the wedding."

"I am?"

"Yeah, you are." He removed his belt, and she watched his jeans drop to the floor. She didn't need to be told twice about what to do. She sank to her knees, wrapping her fingers around the length.

Just once she wanted to do the complete opposite of what was expected of her.

****

Matthew looked through the list of ingredients that Holly had given to him. There was unsalted butter, cocoa powder, and all kinds of other crap to make a wedding cake. They had until this weekend to do a cake, and they were in mega baking mode.

With Beth's sudden change of plans, he was the only one available to head to the grocery store to gather the ingredients.

His cell phone went off, and he answered it.

"What else have you forgotten?" he asked.

"We're doing all the catering now. I need meat, Matthew. Pretty much everything that you see, put it in the trolley. Duke's going to meet you out front with the truck to bring it all back."

"You're starting now?"

"We're planning everything now. You're a star, Matty."

He rolled his eyes, hanging up the phone, and rounded the corner, crashing into another trolley.

"I'm so sorry," the woman said.

Matthew recognized that voice, and looking at the woman he'd crashed into, he stared at Luna, the girl he had the pregnancy scare with.

"Matthew," she said, and he watched as she withdrew into herself.

"I'm so sorry, I wasn't watching where I was going, and Holly was talking."

"Holly's with you?"

"No. She's sent me to the store with a long list. Beth, she's getting married. Daisy's sister is getting married, and well, everything going crazy, and I'm rambling on, and I'm really embarrassed right now, so I'm going to be quiet."

Luna chuckled. "It's my first time back since college. Folks sent me out shopping."

"You look good."

Her cheeks heated. "Thank you, I think."

"I'm really sorry about what happened."

"Don't worry about it. You were a lesson that I needed, and I've been better for it."

"A lesson?" he asked, frowning.

Once again her cheeks went a deeper shade of red. "Yeah, um, you taught me to never trust a guy. I'm always a little hesitant now, and I no longer tutor. Tutoring is off the menu for Luna." She chuckled.

He didn't see it.

Luna was his one biggest regret.

"Anyway, lovely to see you, and I'm sorry we

parted on bad terms—"

"I wish you'd been pregnant," he said, startling them both.

"What?"

"I think about it all the time. I wish I'd gotten you pregnant, and that I'd have a reason to keep you."

Tears filled her eyes, and she looked down. He saw her wiping them away. "You slept with everyone, Matthew."

"I was an asshole, and fucking stupid. I see that now, and it's my error. I want you to know that not getting you pregnant would be my biggest regret."

"We're still kids."

"Yeah, we'd have made awesome parents." Matthew moved past her, and neither of them stopped each other as they passed on by. "If you ever change your mind about getting to know me, I'll always be in Vale Valley."

"Don't you go to college?"

"Yeah, but I come back here every chance I get." He quickly scribbled his number down, tearing off the piece of paper. "Call me any time."

She took the paper from him, and Matthew had no choice but to walk away. For the first time in his life, he understood rejection. Not once did Luna say that she wanted to be with him.

This was going to be a moment he remembered for the rest of his life.

****

"Beth and Knuckles are about to get married, and you're telling me that somewhere out there is my real father?" Holly asked.

Duke stood beside his wife, knowing she was struggling to hold everything in. This wasn't supposed to happen, but Duke couldn't keep this big of a secret from his wife.

"We wanted to tell you," Sheila said.

"No. If you wanted to tell me, you would have done. This man, this Abelli, he's my father?"

"Yes."

Holly shook her head. "You know what, this is not happening today. I'm going to the church, I'm going to be a bridesmaid, and I'm not letting you two's mistake ruin my friend's day."

"Sweetie," Sheila said, reaching for her, but Holly pulled away.

"No. This isn't something easy for me to digest. Duke's been worried about this … man, and now that man turns out to be my father." Holly shook her head. "This is the same man that got Winter hurt. This is not happening."

Duke followed his wife down the long path toward the waiting car. Once inside, Holly leaned against him. "It's bad, isn't it?" she asked.

"Not that bad."

"How do you figure?" Holly asked.

"You're Abelli's long-lost daughter."

"Great, a daughter to the mafia. Fucked up."

"Maybe he'll be more considerate to the club seeing as he's found you."

"Found me? No one has found me, Duke."

Duke held his hand out. "I reached out to Abelli."

"Against Clinton?"

"No, against Russ."

"What did you do?"

"I organized a meeting, him and me. I want to take you with me."

"This is dangerous."

"The fallout from Winter and Russ could kill the entire club. Please, see it from my side."

Holly sighed. "We've had too good a life."

"That life is not over. I have a plan, babe. I always have a plan."

Epilogue

Three months later

Beth waved at Knuckles watching as he came out of the ocean. They had been married for three months, but with commitments, and club crap, they had only just gotten away on their honeymoon.

Knuckles ran toward her, and she giggled as he lifted her up in his arms and carried her out to the waiting sea. She laughed, screamed, and tried to get away, but he dropped her down into the water before she could.

"You monster," she said, swimming toward him, and trying to duck him under. He couldn't let that happen, and she ended back under. He released her, and rushed out of the ocean, and she charged after him.

Throwing herself into his arms, Knuckles twirled her, pressing his lips against her.

Once they finished messing around, Beth collapsed to the sand, panting for breath. "Are you going to tell me what the call was about with Duke?" she asked.

Beth had only heard one side of it, but she knew it was bad. Knuckles hadn't stayed around long, rushing outside into the open water.

"Shit's going down at the club, and he wanted to warn me."

"We're not due back 'til next week."

"He wants me back early for the club. He needs me there."

Beth let out a sigh. Since her marriage, the club had been … tense. They had discovered that Holly and Duke had met with Abelli, along with a few other interesting facts. Beth felt sorry for Holly, as she had just realized the man she'd been calling a father, wasn't him.

"What do you want to do?" she asked.

"I want to stay and enjoy my honeymoon. The club though, I'm needed there."

Resting her chin on his shoulder, she smiled up at him. "I've already booked he tickets, Knuckles. I told you I'd never make you pick between me and the club, and I won't do it now."

"We're going back home?" he asked.

"Home is wherever you are, and if that is on a beautiful romantic beach, in a clubhouse, our apartment, or a dump, providing I'm with you, I don't give a damn."

He pulled her into his arms, and she giggled. "How did I get so lucky?" he asked.

"Maybe you've been asking for me in your dreams, and they were finally answered."

Knuckles pulled her down, kissing her. Their relationship would survive anything. She loved and trusted him. Beth would do anything for him, and he anything for her. Sometimes the club would take priority, but it would be with her he slept, with her that he talked, and with her that he spent the rest of his days with.

For the rest of their lives.

The End

www.samcrescent.com

BESTSELLING BBW ROMANCE
SPICY ROMANCE FOR REAL WOMEN

SAM CRESCENT

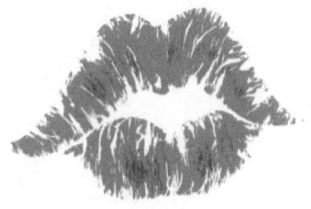

EVERNIGHT PUBLISHING ®

www.evernightpublishing.com